CAN I HAVE YOU?

JA'NESE DIXON

PUBLISHING

CONTENTS

I'm trapped in a beautiful prison. Ryan's badge keeps me submissive long enough to formulate a plan. Because I can't stay.

So, I do the unthinkable running back to the only place I consider home, Madison Grove, with him hot on my heels. Then I find Mac again, and he makes my heart ache for more, thanks to his small-town charm and quiet determination. But I'm on borrowed time.

I'm trapped between an obsessed cop and an ex-Marine, outrunning my destiny or finding my forever or both. Because I can't trust love.

Or can I?

CHAPTER ONE

"Dez! Get your ass out here. We want another round."

I shake my head, exhaling the pent-up energy in my chest. I complete the message to my sister Faith while I consider my next move because I don't want to go out there again.

Ryan and his *boys* yelled and cheered for the past two hours while watching the football game. But with each quarter they got more agitated, questioning the referee's rulings, berating the owner, and cursing the coaches as their beloved team loses the game. I hear the rustle of clothes.

Oh hell, he's coming back here. I stand dropping my phone in my back pocket. I yank the hem of my shirt out to hide it. He doesn't know about her or this phone. I cross the room, pausing in the doorway to listen again.

The last thing they need is another round, but Ryan is better handled passed out than awake.

I slip out, walking past the media room, and slow down at the sight of their shocked faces. That room is my favorite in the house. Ryan had spared no expense when decorating from the flooring to the high vaulted ceiling. He hired an interior designer and customized everything, but it's the entertainment center with surround sound that has their eyes glued to the screen.

"Ahhh man! Did he just fumble?" Ryan snaps to his feet, pointing at the life-size player then his angry eyes find mine. "Why are you draggin' your feet like we have all fuckin' night?"

Let me get his damn beers. I move faster, entering the kitchen. I flick on the light, his eyes watch my every move. I can't piss without him standing outside the bathroom since my last runaway attempt.

"Touchdown!" The roar of their cheers echoes through the house as the rumbustious guys get louder. I glance over, and they're dabbing and congratulating each other like they made the pass.

Play nice, Destiny. I lower my head into the refrigerator. The sweet aroma of melon greets me. I push air out my mouth in anguish because I've extinguished all of my plans, now I'm left with waiting for an opportunity to arise. The only way I'll get out of here alive is to make Ryan believe that he can trust me.

I push around the beverages and condiments on the top shelf and find three beers left. Then I open the bottom drawer spotting the grapes. I pop one in my mouth, slamming it shut. Nope, only three. And there's three of them.

I stay folded over and lift my eyes to peek over the top of the refrigerator door. Ryan is sitting in the recliner focused on the game. Mike, his partner, is talking in his ear, pointing back and forth at the screen as if discussing a play. I reach inside, keeping my eyes trained on Ryan, and remove a beer. I used the tip of my nail and slide it under the tab, slowly releasing the air from the can.

Once the hissing stops, I hold my breath, pressing the tab. The faint crack of the can opening sends my gaze across the room again. He didn't hear it, I sigh in relief.

Hurry, Destiny.

I extend my hand with the opened can to the sink. I'm lightheaded because I refuse to breathe. He can't see what I'm doing or he'll... The options flash before my eyes, and none of them are ideal or pretty. So, I keep him in sight while letting the malt liquor flow down the drain.

"Dez!" he yells, impatience laced in his tone.

My heart drops as his opal green eyes glare over the banister separating the kitchen and the media room. I used to love his eyes. He'd turn me on from the mere sight of them. Then add the chiseled body and his smile. He's all American as apple pie and football. Then he changed.

The can is nearly empty, and I'm praying he can't see my arm because this beer is my escape plan. "We only have two beers left." My voice is barely over a whisper.

God, please don't let this man kill me and let his friends watch him do it.

"Ryan, did you see that pass?" Mike asks.

Ryan looks away, and I hurry, tossing the empty can into the trash.

"I can run to the store and get more." I train my voice to be even and void of emotion.

His eyes spitfire but I don't break eye contact. He's held me hostage in this house for almost three weeks. What makes it worse is knowing they're all cops, and I can't ask a single one of them for help. I've tried, and it resulted in Ryan nearly putting me in the hospital. He knows how to push it far enough to make a point but not far enough to end my misery.

"Nice try. Bring them. And make me a Jack and Coke."

Hell. I drop my head. It's going to be a long night. I move quickly around the kitchen. I take the beers to the guys who mumbled their "thanks" before retracing my steps back to make his drink. I need his favorite glass.

I open the smoky grey cabinets and spot it on the second shelf from the top. He knows I can't reach that shelf. I inch onto my tiptoes trying to use every bit of my five-foot four-inch height to obtain the old-fashioned crystal tumbler. I stretch with a slight thrust of my left leg and used my middle finger to inch it toward the edge.

"Here let me help you with that." Mike startles me, reaching around me.

"I got it—"

His arm brushes across my breast, and I stumble back hoping Ryan didn't see it. But the daggers he's shooting in my direction let me know my hopes went unheard. Rage churns in my gut because I can't catch a fuckin' break. And Mike knows Ryan is crazy.

"Thank you." I push through my clenched teeth. "Did you need something?"

"We need more chips." His eyes sparkle with mischief as he places the empty glass bowl on the marble counter. Mike's x-ray eyes make my skin crawl. What is it with jerks? They all flocked together.

"I'll get it," I offer in my nicest falsetto to get him out of the kitchen. Mike's an asshole and a coward like the rest of them. His attempt to get a little feel will result in a fight tonight.

"Dez!" Ryan's tanned skin is flaming red.

"I'm coming!" My response is harsher than I intended, and his arched brow tells me so.

I grab the bottle of flat soda and pour it into the glass, adding the whiskey with an extra flick of my wrist. He turns back to the game, and this is my shot. I release the powder from one, two, three capsules into his glass. Then I add one more to give me a head-start. I stir the concoction with my finger and add a little extra whiskey to mask the flavor of the sedative.

I can make his favorite drinks and meals with my eyes closed. Because in the beginning, all I wanted was to make Ryan happy. To make Ryan love me. Now, I wish Ryan would just let me go.

I head to the family room, stopping to circle back for the chips. I give Ryan his drink.

"I saw that." He yanks my wrist towards him, bringing me closer. I flinch, bringing my arm up to protect my face. I swallow as tears gather in my eyes. He pushes me away, and the guys laugh as I stumble to the floor.

I won't give him the satisfaction of seeing me cry. Instead, I crawl backward out of his reach and cling to the silent clock counting down in my head. I'm busting out of this place tonight, and I'm never coming back, I declare with every ounce of my being.

"Get your ass back to the room."

I ZERO IN ON THE ANIMAL PRINT SHOES IN THE BOTTOM OF the closet. I used to love going to the zoo. But after experiencing life in captivity, I sympathize with them. To pace back and forth with freedom so close, yet so far.

I scan the room, the bare white walls, the California king-size bed, the fancy wooden blinds. Thirty-two of them. I've counted from top to bottom. The counting makes the waiting bearable.

Every footstep down the hallway triggers my fear of Ryan rounding the corner since the game ended less than an hour ago. But they've been sitting around drinking and talking while the commentators recap the game.

Ryan had seven beers, three mixed drinks, and four sleeping pills. He should be dead on his ass, but he's awake quoting player stats. Maybe I should have added one more. Then the sound of the commentators cuts out.

They're leaving.

I tiptoe to the doorway and peek around the corner. They are sliding back into their holsters, the light shines off their badges, and it disgusts me. The moment they head to the front door, I move back, placing a hand over my racing heart.

Think, Destiny.

Praying didn't help. Running didn't help. The police didn't help. What else am I supposed to do? Nothing is coming. I'm out of options.

I drop my head back, bouncing my fist against my thigh as the ceiling fan spins in circles. It's an ideal metaphor for my life, round and round. But I always find myself back in this same space.

On my own.

I couldn't depend on my mother, the system, Ryan, my sisters. I have to save myself. The alarm deactivates, and I scramble side to side frantically looking for a weapon. Ryan will blame me for Mike, and I'm not going down without a fight.

"Night, Dez," one of them yells from the living room.

"Night. Drive safely."

I open a few drawers and search beneath our bed. They've had enough alcohol tonight to issue several DUI citations to each other. None of them should drive, but I'm staying out of it. I have enough problems of my own.

I pick up a stiletto, testing the weight of it in my hand. That will only piss him off. I toss it back into the closet. My Kitty! I glance around the room, looking for my pink backpack. I found the plastic self-defense weapon online. But it's in my bag.

I go back to the doorway, first assessing Ryan. He looks exhausted. His eyes fight to remain focused on Mike, repeatedly yawning while standing near the front door. And I see my pink backpack beneath the end table.

Fuck! How stupid can I be? I buy the weapon and leave it out there.

"Man, don't forget to swing by and pick me up tomorrow." The slight slur in Ryan's voice gives me hope that the pills are working.

"I got you. I'll give you until two," Mike says, and they laughed in their drunken stupor.

"You better make it three." Ryan stumbles back a little.

"All right, man. Get some sleep. Goodnight."

Ryan closes the door behind Mike. He flicks the bolts, turning out the lights before stalking in my direction.

"You should be tired of this fight." His eyes meet mine alert.

Icy fear twists my heart, I'm tired of living in a constant state of panic. I walk backward until my back is against the wall.

"Babe, why don't you go to bed? I'll clean up out there."

Please, drugs kick in.

"Oh, I'm babe now, but what about when you were pushing up all on Mike a few minutes ago."

"I didn't push up on Mike!" I match his tone, and his hands reach for my neck.

"Don't you know I'll—"

Ryan lunges for me, and I shift my weight between my feet better than a running back with a linebacker hot on my heels as I dart into the bathroom. Locking the door behind me. I collapse, unable to catch my breath. I can't let him in this bathroom.

Bang. Bang. Bang. The hinges shake, and the wood sounds as if it will give in to his protests.

"Open this got-damn door."

Bang. Bang. Bang. I move to the wall, sliding down to the floor, pulling my knees to my chest. I place my phone beside me and watch the minutes pass as his banging dies. Thirty-seven minutes later, the house is silent. I stop breathing and listen for any sign of movement outside the bathroom.

I hear nothing. I dry my face with the hem of my shirt and place my ear to the door. I hear the hum of the refrigerator and the ticking of the grandfather clock in the formal living room. But I don't hear Ryan. We're at a stalemate in this relationship.

I run. He finds me. I run again. He sends his buddies to drag me back to this prison that's sucking the life out of me.

I hold my breath, slowly turning the lock on the faded gold doorknob. I positioned my foot against the door to give myself leverage if he decides to force his way inside. I exhale letting the air quietly pass over my lips and hold my breath again, this time listening for sounds around me. Listening for Ryan.

Dr. Jekyll *or* Mr. Hyde.

Crowned prince or the Beast.

Ryan goes from sweet to nasty in the blink of an eye, and with me, he seems stuck on evil. The further I run, the harder he fights to make me stay.

All of this in the name of *love*.

I shake my head. How foolish am I to believe he built this house for me? That he paid for my college education to make me happy? That he moved us to the suburbs to have a better quality of life?

I'm the biggest fool to exist, and I want out.

The sound of soft snores coming from the bedroom. I release the pent-up air and relief washes over me. The time on my phone shows 2:17 a.m. Mike would be around to pick up Ryan for their shift in forty-five minutes.

I shove the phone in my pocket, moving as quietly as haste will allow. I stop in the doorway of the bedroom. Ryan's spread out across the bed passed out. The Sonata and whiskey cocktail should keep him knocked out for a while, but it doesn't account for Mike.

I run to the family room and get my backpack. I throw whatever I can stuff inside. Then I notice his wallet, keys, badge, gun, and handcuffs on his nightstand, as usual. I use the cuffs on him and take the keys to his beloved truck. It's time to blow this joint.

IT IS A LITTLE AFTER FOUR, AND I CAN'T GET AWAY FAST enough. Unlike my past attempts, I didn't have months to plan my escape this time. I had to improvise and recall all the ways he'd caught me before in a matter of seconds.

I change lanes, glancing in the rearview mirror. There's a cop car on the shoulder of the road. I keep my eyes rapidly bouncing between the speedometer and the rearview mirror. I slow down because I didn't come this far to get stopped for speeding, plus the moment they run his tags they'll know the truck belongs to a cop.

I grip the steering wheel so tight my nails dig into my palms. Once the coast is clear, I turn on the music to a faint whisper to fill the space of the cabin. I smile, but I can't celebrate. The first forty-eight hours are crucial. The highs and lows of tonight have me ready to sleep for hours, but I need to keep driving.

Gum will help. I reach for my backpack on the floorboard. I packed a few belongings. *Wait, did I get my journal?*

"Oh, no!" The truck swerves, and I struggle to

compose myself. I lean over and grab the bag from the floorboard. I use a hand to search for my notebook.

"Please don't say I forgot it. Please..." I plead, but no one can help me.

My journal has all my notes, phone numbers, email addresses, my log. He can't have that book. I keep an eye on the road, while frantically exploring the contents of my old pink backpack.

I feel my wallet, jeans, toiletries. I pat around, careful not to stab my finger with My Kitty at the bottom. Suddenly my hand brushes against a cardboard-like texture. I lift it out of the bag. Thank God I have it. I yank the top of the bag to make the contents fall to the bottom, and I toss the journal back inside.

Where am I going?

I cleared out his wallet, leaving his credit cards. I can hear him and the guys laughing at a case they broke because someone was stupid enough to use a credit card. Credit cards and cell phones. But luckily, he took my cell phone, and I bought a new one during my last escape. So, Ryan doesn't know about my phone.

I have enough money to fill up the tank of his Dodge Ram once, maybe twice, which means I can't go far. My heart selects the destination, a place Ryan knows nothing about.

A real smile crosses my face as I signal to exit the highway. I'm going to Madison Grove.

"THERE SHE IS. COME TO ME ..." I LEAN CLOSER TO THE computer monitor. I searched high and low, and with the click of my mouse, she's all mine.

Click.

"Yeehaw!" I pump a fist in the air, pleased with my conquest.

"Yeehaw!"

I chuckle as Dad's voice echoes down the hallway. Classic cars are my hobby, my business, my passion. It started with toy cars, moved up to model cars, and now I'm hanging with the big boys, buying the real thing.

My purchase today is a 1994 Chevrolet Corvette. I pull out my clipboard with the list of American muscle cars I intend to buy for my passion project, Mac's Muscle Cars. I proudly check the 'Vette off the list because this beauty is for me.

I glance at the time, I need to hit the yard before the temperature heats up. I stand and stretch my back and shoulders, loosening my tight muscles after sitting folded over my computer. The private owner and I emailed and messaged for about a week making this deal happen. I look side to side, filling my tiny office to capacity. My six-foot frame means I can touch the tops of all the doorframes and if I stretch wide enough, I can brush the four walls of my small office while sitting at my desk. Hence, one of the reasons I'm trying to get Dad onboard with remodeling this place.

I survey my desk and go back, placing the mouse back in the center of the Reese & Sons mousepad. I drop the pencil in the holder just left of the computer stand. Something is off-balance...my mug. I move it a little to the right to sit centered on the coaster. Satisfied, I push the chair beneath the desk and walk out my office into the chaos my father calls *our* family business.

I returned home after serving twelve years in the Marines to become the "& Sons" in *Reese & Sons* since my younger brother Christopher wants nothing to do with the family junkyard business. I have plans to upgrade our business, but first I have to get this place organized. I can't think, let alone work, in Dad's clutter.

"Dad, when are you going to clean this place up." My father, Reese, stands in his regular spot behind the counter separating the waiting area from our private offices.

"Stop being a grouchy old man and help me find what I'm looking for," he demands, not bothering to look my way.

I cross the distance, stepping over a large cardboard box. I stop next to him and look inside... "What are you looking for, Dad?"

"The spare key to the safe." He puts the box back on the shelf beneath the service counter and reaches for a white basket. Dad pushes the contents around and discovers several keys. He shakes his head before putting the basket back on the shelf.

"Brittany probably misplaced it. Here, use my key, and I'll look for it later." I pass my keys. We keep the important insurance documents and money waiting for deposit in the safe since we rarely handle large amounts of cash. But our recent addition of a consignment lot with "as-is" cars, trucks, RVs, and boats, has increased our cash flow since we give people a discount for paying with cash.

Dad heads back to his office, returning a few minutes later with a title and set of keys. I place my keys in my pocket, trying to find the right way to get him on board with my plans. But he's a creature of habit and changing the office seems like a waste of time to him. I see it differently.

He kicks a box to move around, and I groan. "Dad let me clean this place up."

"Will it get you off my back?" He stops with his arms hanging at his sides. I nod. "Then do it."

"Really?" We've been going round and round since I had the blueprints commissioned.

"Yes, just don't touch my office and don't turn this place into a highfalutin' shop with espressos and mixed drinks. None of those ten-dollar coffees for our place Mac."

He thinks the town took a turn for the worse the moment fast food restaurants and "high dollar coffees" came to our small country town, Madison Grove.

"Yes, sir." He starts his slow walk back out the door. "Love you, Dad."

"Yeah, yeah." He throws a dismissive hand my way and disappears through the doorway.

"Yeehaw!" I toss my hat in the air and catch it. I don't have a cosign this time, but I don't need it. I've scored a car and got Dad on board with making changes. This day is getting better by the minute. Now to find someone to clean the place up, before he changes his mind, or my mother gets wind of his approval.

According to Dad, the sun rises and sets on Nancy McKenzie, and there's no defying her although I can't recall the last time I've seen her around here.

Dad started Reese Junkyard as a small business over

thirty years ago with only two acres of land. They slowly increased to ten acres adding the "& Sons" once I decided to retire from the Marines last year. Then earlier this year I purchased the adjacent lot with twenty acres to give us plenty of room for this new wave of Reese & Sons.

I make a call to the architect to schedule a meeting to revisit the blueprints because it's time to upgrade inside and out. A larger office, new computers, a custom database to catalog our inventory, and most of all, I plan to reorganize the layout of the junkyard.

Dad returns with sweat glistening on his forehead. "It is still hot out there! And its September. We can forget having a real winter." He walks back to the counter and pulls out the consignment ledger.

"I need to get moving. I'm headed out to work with the crew. I want them to get the paths identified, and maybe we'll get some of the aisles established. What time is Brittany going to grace us with her presence?"

Dad shrugs. "Your guess is as good as mine."

"Why did you hire her? She never shows up on time, she leaves early, and she takes cigarette breaks every half hour."

"Your mom." He takes a drink of his sweet tea from his mason jar and sits on his stool.

I shake my head. Dad makes the statement as if that alone explains why we pay a woman to drink all our sodas and play on social media all day. I have to pick my battle on this one. I got him to agree to the renovation. We'll have to address the issue of Brittany another day.

I push the door open, and the steam from outside assaults me. I lower the rim of my baseball cap and turn back to Dad. "Oh, and I have a car delivery scheduled for today. Call my cell when she arrives."

"Okie doke." He tips the glass my way, and with a two-finger salute, I'm out.

I close the door, crossing the parking lot, walking to the golf cart. I need to mark off the areas for the crew. I sit behind the wheel, and a loud pop cuts through the steamy silence. I skim the space around me. The parking lot is empty. I walk to the country road in front of our land to offer a hand or extend our services.

We're the only ones around for a good stretch. There's about thirteen miles from Main Street and twenty from the highway running between Dallas and Houston. I stop at the edge of our drive, looking both ways.

I lift a hand to shield the sun from my eyes. I need to go back and get my cowboy hat, because this one won't cut it out in the yard. I walk toward the crew cab Dodge Ram rolling to a stop. I see the problem from here, the back left tire is flat. It must be a traveler passing through because I know most of the cars belonging to locals.

I walk over to the shiny truck. It's definitely not a

work truck, from this angle I can't see a lick of dirt, mud, or grime on it. A petite woman hops out with two jet black French braids running down the length of her head. They dangle forward as she inspects the tire. I take my time to appreciate the view as her backside faces my direction.

I push that thought aside. It's been over a year since I've entertained a woman, a few since I've been in a real relationship. My job in recon made it hard to remain honest with my female companions, so, to keep from lying, I stayed away from commitments. But the heat lingering in my body for the legging-clad beauty makes me take a mental note. I need to change that, and soon.

I'm not a Marine anymore. I'm a civilian living a regular life and regular should include more than junk, cars, and hanging with Dad and Christopher.

"Morning, ma'am. Can I give you a hand?" I stop a few paces behind the truck bed. It sure is a large truck for such a small woman. Up close I'm impressed by the polished exterior decked out in chrome.

She turns, and I'd know that face anywhere. Destiny Mitchell.

"Ethan McKenzie." A slow smile crosses her face. Her tawny brown skin matches her hazel feline eyes. She was always a looker. Destiny props a hand on her hip, "Mac, what are you doing here?"

I feel the smile crawl across my face. "I live here.

Thank you very much. What about you? Are you here visiting or just passing through?"

"A little of both until this decided to slow my roll."

In a flash, it's like I doused cold water on her. I want her smile back. I step closer until she turns her head upward to meet my eyes.

I wink. "Well let's see if I can get another view of that smile of yours."

"STOP FLIRTIN' AND HELP ME."

Mac laughs and moves closer to the truck.

They didn't call him Mac for nothing. He was always a flirt. He updates me on his parents and the junkyard while removing his flannel shirt. His muscles bulge as he folds it, tossing it over the side of the truck. I step back to give him room to inspect the tire, standing close to a man, any man, sets Ryan off. I cross my arms, remembering Ryan is a nonfactor.

Mac is staring at me, waiting. *What did I miss?*

"Where's the spare?" I ask, hoping he doesn't notice that I zoned out. I need his help because I have no idea how to change the tire. Ryan never let me drive his truck, and he took the car he bought me months ago.

"It's underneath. Did you just get this truck? She sure is a beauty." He walks around to the passenger side.

"Uh...no. It's a loaner." The words stumble out. I need to pay attention and figure out how I'm going to explain my arrival.

"Are the doors unlocked?"

I open the driver's door and disengage the locks. He opens the door and fiddles around until he removes a bundle from beneath the seat.

"Well, I'll be. Who knew that was there?"

"I did." Mac flashes the smile that had all the girls giggling in high school.

"Ha, haha." I shake my head at the mischievous wiggle of his eyebrows. I'm curious to see what he does next. I step closer, leaning against the seat to get a better look because it would have taken me ages to uncover it. That or a hundred YouTube tutorials.

Mac fiddles with three black beams until they made a "t" shape. "So, how long are you planning to visit?" he asks as we walked to the back of the truck.

"I'm not sure. I want to visit, save some money then maybe travel a little."

I figure that Mike found Ryan a few hours ago. That makes me nervous. I need to get rid of this truck and plan my next move. But I have two things that make me hopeful that this time I'll succeed, the fact that Ryan doesn't know much about my sisters or my life in Madison Grove.

"So, tell me, who stayed and who left sweet ole'

Madison Grove?" I change the subject, and graciously Mac fills me in on old friends from high school, the town upgrades like the renovated Main Street, and the new businesses booming in town.

He lowers the spare and before I know it, Mac has me ready to hit the road again.

I yawn and glance over his shoulder as a flatbed tow truck backs into the parking lot behind us.

"Is that still your dad's place?" He nods. "Man, it sure seems a lot bigger than I remember."

"Yeah, that's because we've expanded the place." He bundles the tools back and places them securely beneath the passenger seat. He closes the door and turns to me.

I get a good look at Mac. His eyes hold the gleam of wisdom. He was a playboy in school, but he was always kind to my sisters and me. Kindness is a trait I never quite valued until I found myself steeped in a man's jealousy, impatience, and uncontrollable anger.

"You told me about everyone but Kenneth. How is he?" They were inseparable in high school.

"He's no longer with us." The sadness that passes over his face tugs on my heart.

"I'm sorry, I didn't mean to—"

"No worries." He rubs his hands together, looking at the grime from handling the tire. "Make sure you replace this tire. You don't want to drive around without a spare." He gestures to the tire in the bed of the truck.

"Mac..."

We stand in awkward silence. "I need to head back. Are you all good?"

"I think so." I nod, hating that I ruined the moment. I open the door to get back in the truck.

"Let's do lunch or something before you leave." He offers.

"I'd like that."

"It was good seeing you." He smiles and with a two-finger salute turns back to the shop.

I lean against the truck, appreciating his long stride and the fit of his jeans. The abrupt ending makes me want to call him back. From his baseball cap to his worn work boots, I'm sure that man can still make the ladies giggle. Too bad I'm not that lady.

I was never in his league. I was too quiet, too awkward, too poor. But he never made me feel that way. He was always kind. And in many ways, he's always been the standard no one ever met.

I must be delirious because I don't need or want another man in my life when it's apparent I attract the wrong type of men. The issue is either them or me, and I'm not staying around to figure it out. The moment I get enough money to leave the state, I'm blowing this joint, so it's best I stop thinking about Mac and how good he looks in those jeans. Or his smile...yeah...his smile was nice too.

I jump inside the truck, shifting my thoughts to Faith. I crank the engine, and happiness fills me entirely at the thought of her. I haven't seen her in twelve years. I glance back once more, and Mac's standing near the flatbed talking with a man. I shift the truck into gear and head west to see my sister.

CHAPTER THREE

"WELCOME TO MADISON GROVE, DESTINY MITCHELL." I roll down the windows, ducking my head to scan the area around me. It's odd seeing this place again. I raise my foot off the pedal as the speed limit drops to thirty-five miles per hour. This two-lane country road runs right to the major highway. As a teenager, it seemed like the golden path beneath Dorothy's feet, leading to a magic place...Houston or Dallas. But today, it's my path to freedom because instead of running to the big city, I've run home.

I approach the old hangout spot, the water tower. It looks new, or they added a fresh coat of paint. I smile, thinking about my sisters and friends hanging out past curfew drinking beer in that very spot.

The brown sign ahead points in the direction of

Main Street. *Huh.* The old stop sign is now a signal light. I stop, waiting to drive down memory lane.

My sisters, Faith and Hope, and I had been close while growing up. People thought we were triplets, and my grandmother dressing us alike didn't help. I chuckle. We hated it. Little did we know our lives together would be cut short.

The light turns green, and I drive down Main Street. It is the center of Madison Grove. Our lives changed forever when our grandmother died. No one stood up to take custody of us. That left the three of us split between different homes.

Our lives changed in the blink of an eye. We went from teenagers watching Granny—our maternal grandmother, Vivian Mitchell—die to our small family ripped apart. Her death changed me. It changed everything.

That truth still eats at my soul. One minute I had no cares in the world, I was surrounded by love and support, then suddenly I was alone.

My head darts back and forth to see the updates and what's still left. City Hall, the courthouse, the cafe, a new pizzeria. The only bright side was Faith and I lucked out and stayed with families in the area. We attended high school together, but Hope was shipped off to Houston. I wonder if I'll ever see her again.

My heart aches because losing my sisters ripped at

the very fiber of who I thought I was, and I'm still trying to find that girl. The girl that was loving and carefree and not always picking the wrong guys, moving to the wrong places, and not always running with demons at her back.

Ryan's face pops in my head, and I shake him out. He doesn't belong here, not in Madison. I slow the truck to a stop at a standalone structure with its dark red brick and large storefront windows. This is it. I smile so hard my cheeks hurt. The sign reads, "Faith's Boutique," in scripted letters spread the distance of a chalkboard outside her shop. The stylish mannequins are dressed in fashionable spring outfits with sleeveless tops and flowing floral skirts.

I park on the side of the building. The moment I cut the engine, my head falls back. I take a deep breath and close my eyes. I can't contain the happiness bubbling inside me. *Faith did it!*

I can't remember the last time I've felt real happiness. Then fear fills me as a cold whisper in the back of my mind confiscates the moment. *This isn't real or permanent*. Madison Grove is temporary, and kind men like Mac aren't realistic. Men are always nice, in the beginning.

I grip the steering wheel, asking my fluttering heart to embrace this moment. I plaster a fake smile on my face and open the truck door. I jumped down, slamming it closed. There's another sign for Faith's shop on the side of the building. I'm so proud of her.

I walk through the parking lot to the shop. I've spent so many years of my life bouncing around from city to city searching for a good time. I've consumed drugs and alcohol to the point of excess until I stumbled into Ryan at a nightclub. His sandy blond hair and amazing green eyes drew me like a magnet. And knowing he wanted me sealed the deal. Because all I wanted was to be wanted by somebody...anybody.

In the beginning, his overprotective gestures started with small fits of jealousy when other guys asked me to dance. Or if a man smiled at me while we walked down the street. I thought it was cute and it meant he really loved me. It was all cute until I found myself locked in the house for days because he was "keeping me safe" when he was the threat. And he still is.

I push open the door, and the chime of bells above the door fills the shop. Faith is talking with an older woman, our eyes meet, and her jaw goes slack.

"Destiny?"

Her whisper floats to my ears, and I nod as tears sting my eyes. We run through the shop, not stopping until I'm tucked safely in my big sister's embrace. She squeezes me so tight that I feel the love flowing from her heart to mine. I've been running for years, enduring abuse for years, and the reality of knowing it is I who chose that man assaults me. And in the security of my sister's arms, I cling to her, and the dam breaks.

I cry.

Shoulders shaking, body weak, and the agony from my soul manifests a groan and thank God, my sister holds me.

"Please excuse us. Linda, please help Miss Mary."

Faith holds my shoulders tight, pressing me into the warmth of her body, walking us through the shop. We walk into a small office, and Faith closes the door, lowering us to the couch.

"I'm so sorry. I'm sorry…" I wipe at the tears, but they keep coming.

"Are you nuts, Jelly Bean?" She pulls my head up, brushing my hair back. Then she smiles. "Seeing you is like today's my birthday. Or like it's…"

"Christmas day," we said in unison.

I laugh as Faith gathers me back to her. I haven't been called by my childhood nickname in years. Good days to us were always like birthdays or Christmas. Granny supported three kids on social security. So, we didn't have much. But on our birthdays, we always had cake, and on Christmas, we always received three gifts each. It feels good to be someone's gift.

We found each other a few years ago on Facebook. It started with messaging back and forth. Then we shared pictures and pictures led to regular phone calls. We talked most days until Faith began to question me about Ryan.

"So, tell me, how long do I get to hang out with my baby sister?" Faith smiles. She's the same, warm and ready with open arms.

"Not long." I notice a box of tissues on the desk. I grab one and wiped my nose. "I left him, Faith, and I'm not going back. He'll have to kill me first."

"Don't!" Faith covers my lips with her soft fingers. But I mean it, I'd rather die than go back to that prison, than to go back to him.

"And I can't stay here because Ryan *will* come for me." My head shakes at the thought of leading him here. "I can't lead him here. But I didn't have anywhere else to go."

"Where's your book?" Faith asks about my log.

"It's in the truck." When I first started running, it was Faith that told me to track everything, and I've followed my sister's advice.

"Go get it."

I stand, retracing my steps back to the truck. I walk past the women in the shop, and embarrassment burns my cheeks. I fell apart the moment Faith touched me. But I knew returning to Madison Grove was the right thing to do.

I get my journal from my backpack and return to the office. Faith is on the phone, so I sit on the couch to

CAN I HAVE YOU?

wait. Suddenly the heaviness of the night and morning overtakes me. I lay down, folding my arm beneath my head like a pillow.

I'll close my eyes for a few minutes. Faith and I can figure out my next move together. I close my eyes, not worried about my safety. I've been punched, kicked, raped. All sleep isn't peaceful. But today, with my sister near, I gladly let sleep take me.

DESTINY'S EYES BOUNCE, BOUNCE, BOUNCE, AND HER exhaustion wins. I watch her with a heavy heart as she drifts off to sleep. Ryan will not get his hands on my sister. I lost her once, I won't lose her again.

I finish my call with a vendor, and then I call the one person I trust to keep my sister safe.

"Yello..."

I smile and chuckle. He's an old soul. His loyalty and his support over the years have made a difference. I'd love to believe we can do this on our own, but I'm not crazy, and I'm not risking our lives.

"Mac, I need your help."

CHAPTER FOUR

I CRACK MY EYES OPEN, AND THE QUIETNESS OF THE house feels eerie. My eyes fall shut, trying to avoid the brightness.

What time is it? I have work today.

I force my eyes open again and see the ceiling fan above. Last night is clothed in an alcohol-induced haze. I lost count of the number of drinks I had or the time I locked the door behind the guys.

"Dez, close the fuckin' blinds." I groan tossing an arm over my eyes to block out the beams of the sun. I pat the mattress anticipating the warmth of Destiny's soft body, but the sheets are cold. I look beside me, and she's not here.

"Dez…" I call louder this time. "Don't start no shit today. I'm not in the fuckin mood." My mind sweeps the house, listening to all the sounds associated with our home.

The ticking of the grandfather clock. The hum of the refrigerator. The clash of ice dropping from the automatic ice maker. The drip from the broken kitchen sink. I promised Dez I'd call the plumber. I'll do it today.

I hear the normal sounds except her. I don't smell the aroma of coffee or the scent of her body wash. The events from last night flood in my mind.

Destiny running and locking herself in the bathroom.

"Fuck." I need to apologize again. She made my drink too strong. I'll get her a gift after work, a new diamond necklace or maybe an engagement ring.

I roll on my side, but my head protests tightly twisting between my temples. I need another hour of sleep. My eyes slide close then I remember I'm on duty today.

I glance at the clock. It's 9:54. I'm late.

Mike was supposed to pick me up for our rounds. He's probably hungover too. I laugh. Let me call Mike. We have shit to do. I get a whiff of myself and my nose bunches. I smell like a distillery. I guess I'll call him after I take a shower.

I move to sit up and my body yanks sending a tingling sensation through my left arm and shoulder. I pull at it again, turning to see my wrist is handcuffed to the headboard.

"Why that little... Dez! Destiny!"

My head pounds, and I groan in frustration and agony. I try and what does she do...she keeps fuckin' testing me. It's time I teach her a lesson.

"Destiny! Take these fuckin' cuffs off me... Oh, you are going to pay for this one." I listen for movement in the house. But there's nothing. "Dez!"

I frantically slide my free hand back and forth across the black sheets. I feel nothing but fabric and the mattress. I need my wallet to get my cuff key.

How could she?

I lurch forward and steady myself. The dizziness engulfs me, and the musty smell of my armpits mixed with the scent of sweat and whiskey make me nauseous. I gag, and my skin tingles as sweat trails down my spine beneath the t-shirt plastered to my chest.

I fall back to the bed, taking short, fast breaths willing the spinning in my head to stop. Where'd she put my wallet?

I resume my search. Every pat of my hand makes me consider how I'm going to make Destiny pay. I stretch, ignoring the pressure on my shoulder as I use my fingertips to walk across the carpeted floor beside the bed. It's not on the nightstand where I left it, and I can't feel it on the floor. And then I see it on the other side of the room, on the dresser next to my cellphone.

"Fuck!"

My groan is erased by the silent house. The ringing from my hangover is replaced by the racing of my heart. The temperature of my blood increases from a simmer to a boil in disbelief that my Destiny, my Dez, did this. To me.

This time she's gone too far.

What does she want from me? I bought her this beautiful house, and I work hard to give her everything she asks for. And what does she do? She handcuffs me to the bed. This is precisely why I treat her the way I do, chastising and disciplining her like a child. But she'll learn.

She's always flirting with other men. Always dancing provocatively when we're out. Always pushing up on my friends. Most women wish they had a man like me.

I'm pissed, and my head is killing me. Visions of her curly hair and button nose flash before my eyes. The sexy way she smiles at me when we make love. Is asking for her love too much to ask?

"No." I exhale a heavy sigh. "She *will* love me."

The pound of my heart floods my ears, and suddenly I can't breathe. *Calm down, Ryan, Mike will find you.*

Every time I turn around, she's running. Well, I'll

find her, again, and bring her home. And I will teach her to never leave me…again.

Because Destiny's mine. She belongs to me.

CHAPTER FIVE

I STAND BACK, WATCHING THE 1994 CHEVROLET Corvette Coup follow me on the flatbed. I cringe, holding my breath as the flatbed shifts on the unpaved path. What are the chances I finally find her only to lose her? I can see it now, the truck hits a hole then a bump, sending my latest acquisition to the ground. I'm stretching here, but it took ten months of searching to find her.

I roll my wrist, directing the driver this way. In my time home, I've slowly revamped our property. The junkyard occupies the far west end of the property, covering two acres of land. The east side is home to the new warehouse-style facility for auto repairs. We employ a few men and a woman mechanic. Our team's equipped and skilled to handle regular maintenance or extensive auto repairs.

The areas are partitioned by a wide gravel paved road. It allows for the ease of transporting vehicles, customers, and to keep the property decent and in order. Just the way I like it.

The driver creeps to a stop in front of my personal shop at the end of the path.

He swings the truck wide and backs into the space. He steps out and walks to the levels. The hum of the gears lowering the car has my skin jumping with joy. My level of excitement is beyond normal.

"Man, this baby is a beauty." I nod, walking around the car in need of extensive repair with the worn seats and the faded paint. But I agree she was a beauty.

I'll get her back to her original condition. I have time. I rub a hand across the hood feeling for any dings or dents and consider what color I'll paint it, and Destiny's shiny black Ram comes to mind.

I wave as the driver leaves and enter my shop. I will rebuild it and restore it to its best days. I can see myself now, riding on the country roads with the top down. I wonder if I could convince Destiny to join me.

I can't stop thinking about her, from the moment her truck disappeared over the hill. Did she find Faith's Boutique? I'm sure she did, since it's conveniently positioned downtown. Her grand opening is a few weeks away, and I've helped hang displays, signage, and all the "Honey Do" tasks.

Faith really wants to ask Chris for his help, but for some reason she won't. I've learned to keep my thoughts to myself and stay out of people's relationships, or lack thereof.

I shake off the thought of Destiny's jet-black Pocahontas braids and her hazel eyes. Being three years older always made it hard to get to know her. It kept our interactions limited and mostly from a distance. Her warm smile and friendly ways make the loner in me feel normal.

Chris is the people person, whereas I prefer falling back.

Destiny was a cheerleader and boy magnet. I was in ROTC, focused on joining the Marines. We didn't run in the same circles then one day our paths crossed.

The ring of my cellphone brings me back to the task at hand. I smile at seeing Faith's number. She probably has more work for me. "Yello."

"Mac, I need your help."

"Oh goodness, what is it this time?" I chuckle, leaning against the desk. I notice the stack of mail tossed on top, no doubt from Brittany. I balance the phone between my shoulder and jaw freeing my hands.

"Boy, I've known you since you were in diapers." We laughed.

Faith is older. She always uses that diaper line when she wants something, and I always let her think it works. It makes no sense to fight it. I'll end up helping one way or another, that's how things go for Faith. She knows how to get her way, and that's why I leave Chris to his fate because it's only a matter of time.

"What's up?"

"It's Destiny…." The quiver in her voice makes my heart skip a beat. I sit the mail aside and wait.

Faith's my sister, not by blood, and one day she'll be my sister-in-law, once my brother stops chasing money and realize he'll obtain all he desires, and more, with the right people in his corner. He can't get much better than Faith. But until then, I look out for her and now Destiny too.

"Tell me where you need me and when." I listen to Faith as the details of Destiny's dilemma flow out in a single breath.

"I can't tell you everything because she told me in confidence. But Destiny's in trouble and I can't let her return to Dallas. Mac, we have to keep her here and safe." In our long night of working on her boutique, she began telling me about the weight of feeling responsible for not keeping her sisters together. I guess I never gave it much thought since we were kids, and it was years ago. But the pain of their separation is as real today as it was then for Faith.

"What do you need from me? Because you're not

giving me much to go on here, and I can't fight what I don't see."

"I want you to hire her."

"Hire her!"

"What does my business have to do with her safety? I don't run a bodyguard service or an employment agency. I run a junkyard." I run a hand over my face. We already have Brittany who does nothing but sit around smoking cigarettes all day. Will Destiny be another warm body on my payroll? I stand and walk the length of my office.

"You run more than a junkyard. But whatever." I envision the flippant flick of her hand. "I know you want to get rid of Brittany, and you loved my website."

"What does that have to do with this?" I'm confused. I stop and sit in the chair behind my desk, cradling my forehead in my hand.

"Destiny designed my website, and she started my social media accounts. The graphics, the content, all of it is her doing."

"Now you're on to something." I sit back in my chair. I can't fire Brittany because Dad hired her, but I can hire someone to create a website. I like Faith's thinking.

"She is professional, and not just because she's my sister, but she's good Mac. And I figure she can work out there with you and hang low until this issue with her ex blows over."

"So, it was her ex-boyfriend. What else can you tell me about him?"

"That's all. She'll have to tell you the rest. Just know he is dangerous."

"Faith I don't like the sound of this. I can't have some unknown person lurking around causing trouble. I have my folks, employees, and a business to protect."

"Mac, she's my sister." Her voice shakes and the faint sniffle makes me want to grab my brother and solve the issue.

"Have you told Chris?"

"No."

I shake my head. I'm tired of being the middleman between them. "Faith, I do it under one condition."

"And that is?"

"If something jumps off you tell me everything. You can't hit a target shooting in the dark." I've experienced the unimaginable from secret missions to escorting government officials. But I can't protect her from what I can't see.

"I will."

"I'm serious Faith. And she has to agree."

"Okay. Thank you, Mac."

"Don't thank me yet." I smile. "And I want all that snazzy online stuff done to our website too." I have a feeling she'd say yes to anything for Destiny, and something tells me I would too. It's not like I've given her much thought over the years. But seeing her again brought on all the old feelings, the old questions, and a new wave of desire.

"Oh, and one more thing. We need a place to store her truck."

I WORK OUT OF THE OFFICE IN MY GARAGE FOR THE REST of the day. I visit with my team and the contractors before making my way to the front office. But my mind keeps venturing to Destiny Mitchell.

What did I really agree to by harboring her on my land? And what happened that caused her to run back to Madison Grove?

This afternoon I secured the purchase and delivery of four additional cars for my passion project—a '66 Shelby GT350, '68 Ford Mustang Shelby GT500, '70 Oldsmobile 442, and '78 Pontiac Firebird Trans Am. This makes thirty cars counting the ones I purchased today.

I'm about to put Reese & Sons on the map with my personal addition to the family business, a specialty used car dealership with nothing but American muscle cars.

I've invested and saved while away. I set aside two million dollars to make this addition possible. I started with building the storage containers shortly after I returned home. Then I had a state-of-the-art garage built with all the equipment and tools we'll need to restore the vehicles we purchase. Then I hired my crew.

The last step in this process is getting the grounds around the junkyard reorganized. According to the contractor this morning, they should have everything according to my new layout by winter, which means I can start preparing for a grand opening at the top of the year.

It had once been the dream that Kenneth and I shared. We'd invest and become billionaires, retire from the military, and start the shop, together, in Madison Grove. I never expected to bury my best friend before we got this project off the ground. Now I'll have to do it in his memory.

"Brittany, I need to see you." I walk past her. Apparently, she needs a manicure because she's talking on the phone and filing her fingernails at the service counter.

"Uh, huh," she calls back, not stopping the file. "Girl, bye. Let me see what this man wants."

I sit at my desk feeling like a big man in a small space compared to my office in the garage. Brittany stands in the doorway, popping gum, as usual. I've told her a million times how chewing gum and serving clients didn't give a professional appearance. So, she holds the gum in her cheek until she finishes with the client, but as soon as the transaction is complete, she starts smacking again.

"We have a new employee starting tomorrow. I need you to tidy up the office next door. I expect her here around eight."

"I don't get in until ten." She pops a big bubble, cleaning the remnants of the gum off her neon pink lips.

"Then do it before you leave." I sigh exasperated as she pulls her cellphone out of her bra. This is why I let Dad handle her.

"I have ten minutes before my shift is over."

I glance at my watch. It's 15:50.

"You know what, I'll handle it. But you and I need to revisit whether Reese & Sons is the place for you."

"Mr. Reese said I had a job as long as I needed." She cocks her head to the side with a balled fist on her hip.

"The three of us will discuss it together at ten o'clock. Tomorrow."

"You're always so uptight. How about you join me for drinks later?" She twirls a lock of hair around a finger.

In her dreams. I look away from her attempt to flirt. "No, thank you. Instead, I'll see you tomorrow in Mr. Reese's office at ten o'clock, sharp."

Brittany rolls her eyes and heads back to the service counter.

"And Brittany spit the gum out. Now."

Thump.

I cringe at the disgusting sound of the gum dropping in the tin trash can. I hope Destiny's nothing like Brittany because I will lose my mind. And true to her word, Brittany packs up her belongings and leaves eight minutes later.

I'm done too. I'll have to speak with Dad tomorrow. This isn't working. He'll have to just confront Mom.

I gather the pages from the printer for the car I purchased today. I add them to the hanging file. I tidy up my office and turn off my computer.

It's still early enough to get some work done in the garage. I smile, pushing away from my desk. I can work undisturbed, and I'll start by ordering the parts needed for the Corvette. Then I'll order a pizza before calling it a night.

I walk to the front and flick the light switch. I turn the sign directing guests to the machine shop for assistance. I lock the door behind me.

What a day. I hired Destiny, I'm ready to fire Brittany, and it's only Monday.

CHAPTER SIX

I HAVE A JOB. MY FIRST CONTRACT JOB AS A WEBSITE designer, thanks to Faith.

I sit outside the shop, waiting in borrowed clothes. I'm excited and nervous all at the same time. We left the boutique late last night after opening boxes and folding clothes. Talking with her in person reminds me of how much time has passed. I never thought I'd have my sister back. I honestly didn't think we'd cross paths again. It makes me wonder if we'll ever find Hope.

I adjust the coral blouse over the denim capris. Faith ironed out a plan to help me. She is vying for me to stay, but that's not possible. Faith doesn't understand men like I do, especially not men like Ryan.

He's not reasonable. He fixates his mind on a thing, and he's unshakeable. It's what makes him one of the most decorated detectives in Dallas. He always finds his guy, which means like these clothes, I'm on borrowed time. So, I have to keep my plans to leave to myself. It's what's best.

I hear a car drive down the road. I hold my breath checking the mirrors—the rearview and both sides. It passes, and I exhale going back to waiting.

After reviewing my logbook, we took some preventative measures. First Faith insisted we drive outside town, off the major highway toward Houston, and while in motion, she tossed my cellphone since Ryan used my cellphone records to locate me before. Second, we need to hide the truck. I want to ditch it, but it's hard to run with no transportation. For now, hiding it seems like the only option. Then Faith told me about taking the job with Mac.

I estimated having a few weeks at the most. That means my deadline is two weeks. I need to stay long enough to help Faith. That settles it, I'll leave after the grand opening of Faith's Boutique. I take a sip of my coffee and wait for Mac. In my excitement, I left Faith's house early. I went by the cafe in town and grabbed coffee and fresh donuts.

I jump nearly out of the truck at the sound of a vehicle pulling up next to me.

"Sorry." Mac smiles.

I nervously smile back. He climbs out of his old

pickup truck and walks to stand on the other side of the cracked window.

"You're early." His smile matches the warm beam of the sun. His olive skin is more than sun-kissed. I can tell he spends plenty of time outside. His dark hair and dark eyes are as soothing as my cup of coffee.

"I'm excited about my first day of work." I laugh feeling silly. I've been here for at least thirty minutes. Why does the thought of having a paycheck with my name on it make me feel giddy? Maybe it's because it's my first taste of independence.

"Let's get your truck stored away, and we'll get started. Let me get the cart."

I nod, watching him go inside the building. The structure is a one-story building and an average tan color with trees on either side. Mac exits and shakes the keys in my direction. He takes long strides to a golf cart and pulls up next to the truck.

"Follow me. The storage unit is in the back." He drives off, and I follow surprised by the size of the property. From the front, it appears much smaller.

"Pull into Unit 4."

"Okay." I swing out wide then back into the dark space. I roll to a stop shifting the gear into park. Suddenly gratitude floods me. My life is finally moving in the right direction. But the thought I can't move past is Faith and Mac and their generosity.

Yes, she's my sister, and I knew him when we were kids. But that was years ago. Now, here I am depending on the kindness of strangers.

Granted Faith is my sister, but I literally popped up on her doorstep running from a man who claims to love me. A man that kept me from going to the police. A man who just won't let me go.

A man that would....

"Are you okay?"

My eyes fluttered, trying to push away my spiraling thoughts. The interior dome lights turned off, leaving me absorbed in the anonymity of the dark unit. And sitting behind the wheel of Ryan's truck, I can't stop the tears from flowing as regret holds me hostage.

I'm mad at my stupidity of trusting a man who repeatedly hurt me. I wasted years with the heartless coward. And what is worse, I chose him. I spotted him, flirted with him, went home with him. I stayed with him. And I was foolish enough to believe that was love.

My muscles shake as the burden of my life crushes the last bit of hope I can muster. "Can I have a second?"

"Sure, I'll be right outside." Mac turns on the heel of his boots and walks into the sunlight just past the darkness. "And Destiny," he calls out, "it's going to be okay." I can't see his eyes under the shadow of his big Texas cowboy hat. But his words are as close as the breath I hold captive in my lungs.

Dez, you need me.

Who's going to help you?

I'm all you got.

Ryan was there when I had no one. No friends, no family, just us. The sun is over the horizon shining in my eyes. I stare at Mac's shadow as he shoves his hands in his pockets.

I grip the steering wheel, dropping my head between my extended arms. My head dangles, and I exhale the pent-up air, rolling my jaw and shoulders.

I'm tired of running. Tired of always looking over my shoulder. But at least this time I'm not alone. And with that thought, I wipe my face with the hem of her borrowed t-shirt.

I blink, squeezing my eyes shut. "You can do this, Destiny." My voice is flat and unconvincing. But it's all I got. That and time.

I have to evict the thoughts of Ryan from my head. He'd want me to believe I can't do this. But I can, I made it this far. I let out a harsh breath and grab ahold of my weak determination. I'm done with Ryan for good this time.

"I'm not going back."

I toss the truck keys into the glove compartment and close the visor. I slip my arm into the opening of the plastic bag containing the donuts and grab our coffee cups.

Mac and Faith won't regret helping me. I step out of the truck prepared to step into my new life.

THE WEAK SMILE ON DESTINY'S FACE MAKES ME WANT TO fold her in my arms and harm anyone and anything that caused the bleakness to linger in her beautiful hazel eyes. The mere thought of standing between her and her past has me torn, because Destiny Mitchell ran from here, she ran from Dallas, and the truth is she's still running. And I can't let her run off with my heart. It took fifteen years for her to return to Madison Grove. Next time she could leave Texas...Madison Grove...and me in her rearview mirror. And where would I be? Here in my junkyard desiring something not meant for me.

"For you, boss." She extends a cup of coffee towards me.

"I like you already," I tease.

We walk to the golf cart, and I turn the key. She looks over the land, and I wish I had the right words to chase away the ghost of her past. The best I can do is start with making her day a little better. I'm confident I can handle that.

"Let's begin with a tour of the property." And for the next thirty minutes, we ride around the property. I introduce her to the crew in the repair shop, as the tour progresses the Destiny I remember reemerges.

"What's that over there?" She points to the building at the end of the gravel path, shielding her eyes from the sun.

"My shop." I remove my hat and lower it over her two cornrows.

"You repair vehicles too." Her eyebrows peak while she adjusts the hat with two hands.

"Yes, ma'am, I do." I can't resist the urge to pull at one of her plaits. I hold it twisting it between my fingers.

"Oh, don't you start that. Do you remember how you pulled my ponytails as a kid? I hated it." She laughs, and I feel my heart sigh. I drop the braid and turn the cart back around to the front.

"They were always so tempting. And there were two to choose from. What was a curious boy to do?" She shakes her head, and I park the cart. "Now let's get you settled into your office. But I must warn you, it's a mess."

"I'm good with messes." She steps out of the cart.

"Please remember you said those words." I chuckle, reaching for her cup, and toss both of them in the garbage. Then I hold the door open.

"Oh-kay," she mumbles.

We cross the doorway, and she stops. I see the place through new eyes. The boxes from old parts. The stack of invoices on the service counter.

"Let's iron out the details of your job in my office." I gesture to my door down the hall. "And watch your step." I've memorized the positions of the boxes, and although it annoys me, I realize I could have done more to make the office presentable.

"Ouch." Something falls on Destiny's foot.

"I'm sorry." I bend over and lean the pipe back again the wall, my face stinging with embarrassment. "Let me lead the way."

Destiny's a champ because she doesn't say anything negative.

"Please have a seat." I open the door and step inside, pulling out a chair. The walls are pearl white. I have a bookshelf near the window with books showcasing classic cars. Beside my desk, I have an area displaying pictures of my family.

Destiny walks over and picks up a picture of Little Kenny and me. "You have a son?" she asks.

I shake my head. "That's my godson, Little Kenny." I glance away as she returns the picture to the shelf. I need to visit them this weekend. "Let me grab some waters, and we'll get started."

I all but run down the hall to the break room. I pull out a bottle of water and open it, downing half of it before stopping to take several deep breaths. It's still difficult to think about Kenneth. It has been two years, and the pain is as real as it was then.

I finish the water and grab two more before returning to my office.

"Here you go." I pass it over and sit behind my desk. I give her a coaster. "Faith tells me you're great with websites."

"I think great is a stretch. But I love designing websites." In a flash a new version of Destiny emerges—she's a talkative, expressive rendition of herself. She throws around colorful words like "search engine optimization," "meta tags," "customer engagement," and a million other three or four-syllable words that mean absolutely nothing to me. But I love seeing her bloom. So instead of telling her that I have no clue what she's talking about, I sit back and enjoy her presentation.

Her full lips move with her hands flopping back and forth. She draws an imaginary circle in the palm of her hand with an index finger and taps around it. I can't help but wonder what kind of man would want to throw away a shot with her.

A knock on my door startles us.

"Excuse me," I say to Destiny. "Come in."

"Mac," Brittany stands in the door smacking her gum.

"Brittany." I want Destiny to continue, but Brittany seems fascinated by the presence of Destiny in my office.

"It's 10:00."

I glance at my watch, "Correction, it's 10:20."

"Right, well," she had the nerve to look abashed, "Mr. Reese is running late." As if that is an excuse for arriving two hours and twenty minutes late.

"Get started, and I'll be there shortly." Brittany remains in the doorway staring at Destiny. "Destiny Mitchell, Brittany Johnson. She's a friend of the family."

Brittany bucks her eyes in my direction, "Correction, I'm the office manager." She extends a hand to Destiny.

"It's nice meeting you." Destiny stands to shake Brittany's hand.

"Right." Brittany rolls her eyes and walks away, leaving the door open.

Destiny snickers behind her hand. I notice her shoulders shaking as she suppresses her laughter. "Oh, just let it out." And she does.

Destiny laughs until she cries. "I could see the steam rising from your ears. And...and..." She hiccups, trying to catch her breath. "And when she said, 'correction'..." She folds over in the seat after executing a perfect Brittany voice. She is almost hidden from my side of the desk. "Oh, my goodness, wait until I tell Faith."

"I'm so glad I could amuse you." I smile, shaking my head in disbelief. I don't care that she's laughing at me, not when the sight of her smile makes me feel things I thought I missed out on.

"Let me show you to your office." I pass her a

tissue as we go next door. I came back last night and cleared the space leaving the desk, chair, and computer. "I wasn't sure what you would need. We have office furniture in one of the units out back. If you make a list of what you need, I'll have it brought up."

"This is perfect." She walks to the desk and inspects the computer.

"It's only a couple years old. It's Dad's, but he never uses it. He may have turned it on once or twice." I lean against the door with a hand in my pocket, watching as she fiddles with the desktop.

"Mac." I turn to see Dad in the hallway.

"Look who's joining us for a special project." I extend an open hand toward Destiny. Dad shuffles forward, then peeks into the office.

"Destiny? Oh, my Lord, girl, get over here and give me a hug."

She pops up and does as she's told. Dad holds her tight rocking her back and forth. "Well, I must have done something right in my life to get to look into those beautiful eyes every morning," he teases.

Destiny laughs. "Don't make me call Miss Nancy."

"Hey, I can look as long as I don't touch." He wiggles his eyebrows, and I want to push my father out of the room. Flirting.

"Dad, let the woman get to work."

"And don't let Mac hog you to himself." He winks and heads back to his office.

We stand in the doorway for a minute longer. Both of us fascinated by the other. She's less than twelve inches away. I see the flecks of gold in her eyes, the gloss on her lips, smelling the soft scent of perfume. I need to leave before I reach out and trace the freckles across the bridge of her nose. She was always gorgeous.

I take a step back. "Well, there you have it. You've met our colorful crew."

"And a wonderful crew it is." She smiles and her eyes dance with glee, reminding me of rays of sunshine.

"Huh...I'll let you get settled in, and I'll be back in about an hour." I take another step, but I don't want to leave.

Dad's words hit the mark, I too must have done something right in this lifetime because I could stare in her eyes and never tire of seeing them shine. I clear my throat, realizing I'm daydreaming again, which seems to come with having her near.

"I'll see you." I turn to leave, and she reaches out and hugs me, but she quickly jumps back. "What was that for?"

"Just thank you." She walks over to her desk.

"You're welcome."

CHAPTER SEVEN

IT'S OFFICIAL—I'M ONE OF MAC'S COLORFUL CREW members. I'm estimating I'll save a little under three grand to take me to my next destination. A destination I haven't identified. The clock inside my head started the countdown the moment I hit the highway, and it's ticking louder every day.

Working two jobs helps with keeping my mind occupied, though. I work days at the junkyard with Mac and help Faith at the boutique in the evenings. I love every minute of it. Earning my own way, designing a new website, and getting to connect with my sister again. But nights are still hard.

Six whole days have passed and no sign of Ryan. This is the longest I've stayed away. The inside of my jaw is raw from my constant gnawing. I shift my backpack searching back and forth before walking to the shop.

It's Sunday. Why are Sundays always slow and easy? Even the sun seems to linger a little longer off the horizon. The shop parking lot is empty, and there are no cars passing by on the country road. I insert the key into the door. I couldn't sleep so I figured I might as well use the time wisely and the mess in the front service area at the junkyard come to mind.

Thankfully Mac gave me my own set of keys Friday. Faith is working at the boutique around the clock prepping displays, organizing inventory, anticipating her big day. This morning she agreed to drop me off. I glance back at her sitting in the car, waiting for me to get inside.

I push the door open and wave her off. I close the door and deactivate the alarm. Boxes line the walls through the entryway. It's like walking through an obstacle course or a maze to get to my office. I lock the door behind me and pull my hair into a wet ponytail. I should have plaited it. A quick vision of Mac pulling my braid comes to mind. I smile zigzagging to my office.

Mac is more than I realized and much more than I remember. I guess wrapped in my youthful crush he was always larger than life. Now, he's darker, more brooding, not in a way that causes fear but arousal. He seems to appear from thin air with his broad shoulders filling the doorway, a smoky haze in his assessing eyes.

Having him near makes me feel safe, and I haven't felt safe since I slept in a full-size bed with my sisters.

I push him from my mind, sure I'm nothing but a little sister or someone he feels a sense of responsibility for, not attraction. Besides, this is not my resting place. That is somewhere far away from Texas, Faith, and Mac.

The tension in my chest is new because leaving them...*him* seems too soon. But that's the plan, and it's what I do. It's time to start over. Plus, my relationship with Mac is more like a little sister.

I enter my office. The walls are bare void of anything identifying. I drop my backpack in the bottom drawer and turn on some music. I walk back out to the front service area and stand in the middle of a clear patch. I'll start with three piles, a keep, trash, and donate. I wrap a bandana around my head to protect my hair from the dust and get to work.

TWO HOURS LATER, I STAND BACK PLEASED WITH MY progress and head to the break room to put on a fresh pot of coffee. When I return, I nearly jump out of my skin at the sight of Mac standing in the middle of my mess.

"Hey, you." I cover my racing heart. The man is dreamy. *Stop Destiny!* I chide, but I can't help it. I feel like my high school self—eager for him to notice me, to look my way and give me the McKenzie smile.

"Hey, me? What are you doing?" He opens his arms to the new and improved front area. "You know we're closed, right?" His natural smile feels like hot chocolate on a cold night, it's just right.

"I just wanted to make your life a little easier."

He studies me, and he makes me feel things I shouldn't. Not after leaving an awful man behind. I turn back to my task, swallowing my desires to know Mac, the man.

It only took a few days to notice the frustration he experiences walking through the office. Whereas his office is immaculate, and everything has a place. He stores everything where it belongs, down to a single paperclip. I could serve a meal off his floor.

"For this, I owe you big time." He flashes the McKenzie smile, and I'm swooning.

"I like the sound of that." I wiggle my eyebrows, mimicking his favorite gesture. "I think, dear sir, I'm ready to collect."

"What? Already?"

"Yes." And I know exactly what I want to do. "I want to see your shop."

All week I've watched him slip away and work for hours. It's like he closes off the world. Part of me is curious because he's open about all matters concerning the business. He shared his plans for the new cars delivered. One day for lunch, he even took me on a tour of his adjacent land. But the details in his shop remain a secret.

"You don't have to." His face appears guarded.

"Okay."

I'm surprised. I put down the box in my hands and dust off the debris. Then he reaches for me. I stall.

I've intentionally avoided all physical contact with him except that impulsive hug on Monday. I was filled with so many emotions, and the love Mr. Reese showed caused me to overflow with gratitude and Mac was the source. He agreed to help me. He agreed to hire me. He willingly gave me a shot. In a need to express my thankfulness I hugged him, not expecting the surge of electricity that passed between us.

He stands before me like a perfectly chiseled statue with his hand waiting. Mac is an amazing man, and I'm...*faulty*. Part of my musing this week helped me to realize I'm the common denominator in all of the hell I've endured. I picked Ryan. I picked Denzel before him and Lewis before him. The guilt lies at my feet, and my conclusion is obvious, I don't know how to choose the right man I chew on the inside of my raw bottom lip.

"I can stand here all day."

I shake my head, not brave enough to meet his eyes. *What if I'm the fucked up one?*

Not Ryan or Denzel or Lewis but me. They turned on me, and they masked their violence as love. A part of me wonders if that something in me could turn Mac against me too.

I step back, fear, and anger knots inside me.

"Stop. Whatever you're thinking stop and take my hand, Jelly Bean?"

My eyes snap to his, he shows no sign of relenting. Unlike the men before, I know I have a choice with Mac. I stare at his hand then back at his handsome face. His slow smile melts the objections rolling around in my head.

"You're going to pay for that dig," I warn.

Mac's head falls back, and his hearty laugh fills the building. I close the distance between us because he's like the sun on a chilly day...you can't help but stand in the warmth of its rays. I take his hand.

Our fingers lace together. And that thing that is Ethan fills me, spreading up my arm, and settles near my heart. I glance down at the sight of my brown skin intertwined with his tanned skin then I look up and find him waiting. His eyes caress my face.

This feels right, even if I'm not sure whether I can trust my feelings. The best place to start is with being honest with myself. I exhale and admit, I'm attracted to Mac. I'll enjoy the little time we have together before I move on to my next destination. So, I step closer.

"I think your freckles are adorable," he whispers as a gentle finger feathers across my cheek and over the bridge of my nose.

I shake my head and laugh. "I hated them growing up. But now…" I shrug.

"Let's get out of here."

"Lead the way," and a giggle spills out.

"What?" He leads us out of the building towards the golf cart.

"Destiny Mitchell is holding Ethan 'The Mac' McKenzie's hand." He shakes his head and chuckles, releasing my hand to lock the door behind us.

"What am I going to do with you?" He gathers my hand again.

"I don't know, I'm sure we'll come up with something."

<hr />

DESTINY'S HAND IN MINE FEELS RIGHT, SO I HOLD A LITTLE tighter. She leans closer to me, and I wait because when she settles the conversation flows. She has a way of filling in the space like fireworks fill the sky in July. I can't help but stop and stare and be in awe.

I watched her work diligently all week redesigning the website. Thankfully, she kept her comments about my atrocious attempt to click-and-build our old website to herself. She helped at the front counter until Brittany arrived. She escorted customers to the junkyard when Dad wasn't available. She made coffee in the mornings. The more she expressed her selfless acts of kindness, the more I wonder whether I can be trusted with keeping her safe.

We walk the distance to my shop, and I open the door. She steps inside and witnesses my meticulous mess. The walls are lined with my tools. The 'Vette is front and center.

"Why a Corvette?" Destiny walks over to the car and runs her hand over the faded paint, going straight for the jugular. Can I tell her without getting emotional?

She knew Kenneth, and unlike others, she would understand our bond, our brotherhood.

"How about talking over lunch? I brought a couple sandwiches with me."

Relief passes through me. I need a minute to sort through my words. I'm not the expressive man. I'm more of a doer. I get things done, I leave the talking to other people. But her kind patience makes me want to explain.

"Uh...let's go grab something, my treat," I offer, pulling my keys out of my pocket.

"Let me go grab my backpack."

I grab her hand as if it was the most natural thing to do. We stop by the office to get her bag, and I lock up.

The weather is beautiful and not too hot. We'll take the Porsche Boxster.

I lead her over and open the passenger door. She sits swinging her legs inside the low-slung car, another one of my restoration projects. She's not American made, but every man should have a convertible like this. I walk around and climb in beside her.

"How many cars do you have?"

"I plead the Fifth." Destiny laughs as we put on our seatbelts.

I turn the key, and she purrs to life. "I have a small fleet, but many of them will be available for sale. I like the challenge of fixing them up."

She slips a pair of shades from her backpack and tosses it on the floor in the back seat. Then she removes the ponytail from her hair. I watch, fascinated at her curly mane. It's the first time I've seen her hair free.

"I see why you keep it plaited." It's full and spreads across the headrest like a thick black blanket.

She laughs. "Braids make it more manageable. Where are we headed?"

"Do you have plans for the day?" I ask as I merge onto the country road heading toward town. She lowers the shades, and I fight the urge to kiss her.

"No, sir, I'm all yours."

I like the sound of that. "Let's head to Houston."

"Let's." She smiles. "Can I use your phone? I need to call Faith."

I pass Destiny my phone. There's nothing like riding with the top down on an open country road. I make a quick U-turn, taking us away from Madison, and head to the highway.

"Do you mind?" I point to the sunroof as she completes her call.

"Not at all."

I throw the phone in the armrest and drop the top. The cool breeze of the fall morning fills the cabin of the car as we watch the beds of Texas Bluebonnets fly past.

I steal glances at Destiny as her hair dances in the wind. She has a smile of serenity on her face. I increase the speed until we coast at a smooth 75 miles per hour. I toss Destiny a wink, and her laughter is a soothing melody to my weary soul. I wish I had the power to freeze time, to stay in this moment with her because all is right in Ethan McKenzie's world.

I reach for her hand, she holds tight, wrapping her free hand around my forearm.

Yeah...this is perfect.

CHAPTER EIGHT

SIX DAYS.

Six *fucking* days.

Where is she? I fold over the knot in my stomach, rubbing the heels of my hands against my dry eyes. I can't sleep, I can't eat.

What if she never comes back? My jaw locks in agony. There has been no sign of Destiny.

I look at my wrists as if they hold the answers to her departure And my decision not to report my truck missing make my search a challenge but not impossible.

I started with her cellphone. It can take months to get cellphone records, but I have a contact working on it. Destiny thought I didn't know about her little phone, but I did, thanks to the cameras I have hidden in the house. Plus, I found a laptop hidden in the back of her closet.

Thankfully, I let her keep the phone. Now, here's to hoping it will lead me straight to her. My only wish at this stage is that I knew who she kept texting. I'm sure some of them are accounted for, but there are dates and times I'm uncertain about.

In the meantime, I take the jokes from Mike and the guys about finding myself handcuffed to the bed. My skin tingles like a trail of angry red ants covering my exposed flesh.

I brush my forearms, releasing a low growl of frustration. She played me. It must be another dude.

"I'm about ready." Mike types a bit longer at his computer.

It's Sunday, and I'm off. I usually invite the guys over for the game. But it doesn't feel the same with Destiny gone. There are no groceries, and I'm eating out for all of my meals when I finally force myself to eat. So, instead of sitting in our quiet house, I signed up for a little overtime and accompany Mike to Houston. He has a few leads to check out, and I told him I'd ride shotgun, which is better than spending the day alone with memories of her around every corner. Plus, he has a contact that can retrieve information from computers. I tried every possible password match I could think of, but none of them worked.

I pull out my phone, needing to see her face. I swipe through the pictures. Then a few more. Why didn't I notice… I swipe back a few months and even a year. The look is the same. A somber expression with a fake smile. My heart races as the pictures fly past my sight. There must be at least one picture with the gold twinkling in her eyes. After scanning for what feels like an eternity, I toss the phone on the desk.

"You all right, man? Let's do this." Mike stands, grabbing a file from his desk and the laptop. I grab my phone and stand too.

How did I miss it? When did the look of love leave her eyes?

I follow Mike to the unmarked Charger as the images of Destiny occupied my mind. And I can't tell if the burning sensation in my chest is my heartbreaking or my anger boiling like a pit of magma. My gut says it's a healthy dose of both as the lava hits the ice shielding my heart. We reach the car as the rage explodes. I can't hold it back. I send my fist plowing through the window, and it shatters into a billion pieces of glass.

I gather my bleeding hand to my chest. "She better come home soon or I'm going to fucking lose it."

CHAPTER NINE

THE LOW HUM OF THE MUSIC. THE CLEAR BLUE SKY. THE power of this small but powerful car beneath us. I turn my face up, and there's not a single cloud in sight. I flip my face side-to-side to keep my hair from blocking my view. I laugh knowing I'll look like a chocolate Q-tip by the time we reach Houston, but I don't care. And the man next to me...I glance over. How can sitting in an open car could feel strangely intimate?

Mac started the ride, resting our hands on top of my bare leg. Then his thumb began to softly brush little circles on my inner thigh. His touch sends a trail of heat through my body.

My shades block out the sun, but nothing can stop the feeling pooling in my core. Does he know what he's doing to me? His eyes remain focused on the road ahead. His thick hair, high forehead, full jaw. And his lips…

Mac turns as if hearing the war raging inside me. How can I run from one man only to find another? His smoky brown eyes caress my face without moving an inch. I'm losing my shit inside, hoping these shades keep him from seeing the truth.

I'm scared.

I'm scared of what's on my heels, but I'm more afraid of not experiencing this moment with him. Does he know? And is it selfish of me to expose him to the fury of Ryan when Mac opened his life and his business to help me?

His eyes are back on the road, but he brushes farther up my leg. I swallow a gasp. My smooth skin tingles with awareness as his large rough hand covers most of my thigh, inches away from my core. I squirm as my body hums to life.

"You better watch it, Destiny." His eyes dart to me for a second, then back to the highway. The warning hangs between us. I glance down and see I'm not the only one turned on by this moment.

I smile, chewing on my lip, tasting the strawberry gloss. The urge to kiss the salacious grin off his face and tease Mac the way he's teasing me makes me feel alive. And I'm torn in the most delicious and conflicted way.

Men have come and gone. Some decent, most bad.

None have felt like this. Maybe it's my childhood crush reawakened, or that Mac is all man without having to bulldoze his way through life. He just is. Yet the barricade around my heart seems invisible with him. It's like he has the power to shield my jaded heart from the heartbreaks in my past. And I'll be damned if he doesn't stroll his sexy ass right on in without an invitation.

I'm safe with Mac. Safe from harm, and I feel safe to explore a relationship absent fear and manipulation. He's a large man with his broad shoulders and trim waist. His years of service show in his muscular build. But he never uses it as a means of intimidation. If anything, he pulls back, giving me the space I need to lean closer.

Each night when I returned to Faith's house, alone in my bed, the uneasiness and uncertainty of my predicament resurface. Knowing Ryan could be somewhere near means I have to be careful. I'm always looking over my shoulder, jumping at every sound, watching every car that drives past, except when I'm with Mac. That antsy feeling disappears.

I don't get it. I don't understand it. I don't have the words to describe it except to know his presence is like a shield protecting me. It's like nothing I've known before.

I've been on my own for a long time, always bearing the full responsibility for myself. I take care of Destiny Mitchell. But this connection with Mac feels as if he's calling me closer without saying a word as if he's waiting for me to choose him.

The Houston skyline draws near as the traffic slows. Mac and I worked together all week. I redesigned their website in a matter of days with his help and attention to detail. He shared electronic files with the content and images. For hours we huddled around my computer while I made adjustments to match his vision. I basked in the excitement in Mac's eyes when I made suggestions or produced a design that pleased him.

The website is ready to launch. My contract will be complete once I established their social media. *Then what*, a voice in my head whispers.

"Are you ready?"

I blink rapidly and looked around. We're parked in front of a little cafe.

"Where are we?" I push the latch to release the seatbelt, sitting forward, and he is close enough to smell the hint of cologne on his skin.

"My favorite brunch spot." He used the tip of his finger to trace a light trail across my cheek, over the bridge of my nose and doesn't stop until it rests beneath my chin. His eyes stare into mine, and with each second, a furnace heats up.

"Am I underdressed?" His eyes blazed with passion as I fight the urge to close the space between us.

"Destiny Mitchell, you're playing with fire." He pulls

me closer, and I need no additional coaxing as I raise my chin.

"And what if…"

Mac lowers his mouth and captures my words. I surrender to the masterful play of his soft lips, and he nibbles, and teases awake a dormant place within me that lets the light that was wholly Ethan McKenzie inside. A moan escapes, and he responds by threading his fingers in my hair. The passionate exploration of his tongue against mine causes a foggy haze to block out the world. He manages to pull me closer as I cup his face.

He claims me, and I willingly surrender.

In an instant, I know this man, and I want him in every way possible. *What about…* I quiet the voices in my head and push my fears aside because something tells me I don't want to miss the opportunity to love this man. Mac's quiet presence is the balm I need to love again.

Mac ends the kiss. We're breathless. He cups my face, leaning his forehead against mine.

I close my eyes tight. I thought I ran to Madison Grove to leave Ryan, but my heart whispers I was searching for *Mac*.

I'm in trouble…

I feel like a parched man given access to the well of life. The moment my lips touched hers, I'm a goner. It takes every ounce of my willpower to pull away from the lushness of her mouth.

"Let's get inside before they close." She nods, but neither of us moves.

I try to shift my thoughts from the beautiful woman occupying the passenger seat. She's consumed nearly every waking thought since I helped her fix that flat. I sit back, enjoying the taste of her strawberry kiss on my lips.

I look over at Destiny. I felt her studying me for most of the ride. I tried to keep my distance, but she's making it hard for me.

I don't know the status of her relationship or why she returned. I don't know whether she plans to stay or how she feels about me. But the moment she turned her mouth up, I decided I don't care.

I couldn't resist. I want Destiny and the way she returned my kiss said she wants me too. And for now, that is enough.

CHAPTER TEN

WHAT AN AMAZING DAY!

I feel a McKenzie yeehaw in my spirit. The father and son are known to burst out in glee at the oddest moments. Their victory cries ring out in the shop without notice, each one brings a smile to my face.

I return to Faith's house floating. I let myself in and slump onto the couch. It was perfect. Well, not perfect. But pretty close. The traffic in Houston made we wish Mac had a helicopter rather than a sports car. But other than that, today is a day for my journal. I smile, and I wish I could see the goofy look on my face because that's the way Mac makes me feel.

We spent the entire day together. We started with brunch, and from there, we went to the Houston Aquarium. Then we headed back to Madison Grove and stopped by the ice cream parlor before he dropped me off.

"Look at that face." I open my eyes and see Faith heading my way. Her silly grin makes me hold my burning cheeks. Is happiness truly possible after years of misery? The couch shifts as Faith sits on the other end. She curls her feet beneath her. "Stop gloating and tell me already."

I sigh like a lovestruck kid and bat my lashes like butterflies. We giggle like we did as kids beneath the sheets late at night.

"He kissed me."

I stare at the oversized plant perfectly positioned in the corner. I brush my fingers across my lips as if the warmth of his kiss still awaits my touch. In all of my twenty-nine years of living nothing compares to being kissed by Ethan McKenzie. It's probably why he had the girls going crazy.

"Destiny, you know I love Mac like a brother but..."

My stomach drops back to earth. I try to read the look I see lingering in her eyes, but we don't know each other like we used to. I don't like her tone. It's that big sister, motherly...sweetie, I have bad news to tell you voice.

"Are you sure kissing him is wise?"

I look away. I'm not foolish enough to believe relationships are perfect or that butterflies and kisses filled with promise are required. But I'm not ready to exchange my perfect day for reality.

I think about her question while observing the living room. Faith's place is amazing. Her love of fashion transfers smoothly from her home to the boutique and back again. Her couch easily has a million colorful pillows. It gives the feeling of a cozy hug when I sit here.

Faith patiently waits for a response that I don't have. I might as well get this over with, so I drag myself upright and face her.

"What do you mean?"

"You've only known him for a week, and we still have this Ryan situation to deal with. And don't look at me like that. I want you safe first, happy second."

"But it's not your choice or your life." I gather a lilac pillow to my chest. "Don't do this, not today."

Faith stands up, her face clouded with uneasiness, and with a parting glance, she walks back to her room. She doesn't understand.

Tomorrow marks day eight. Eight days away from Dallas. Eight days away from Ryan.

The longest I've stayed away before was five days before he forced me back, kicking and screaming. It's nuts to count each day, each minute, each second. But today is as close to perfection as I can hope for. I won't get too comfortable. I won't let my guard down either. However, I won't let Ryan cancel out Mac, his kisses, and the fact that this time I've secured a job and a place to stay. Because the moment I do, Ryan wins.

I slide my hand into my backpack until I find my journal. Every day is a step closer to true freedom from the life I left behind. I put my journal back and head to my room. I catch a glimpse of myself in the mirror and almost scream.

Mac is a saint, because I'm a mess. Riding in the convertible was amazing, but my hair is a rat's nest. I drop my bag on the floor and get my detangling comb on the dresser.

I sit at the antique vanity. The best way to tackle this job is one section at a time. I gently part my hair down the middle and loosely wrap it into a bun.

"Knock, knock."

I didn't want to talk to Faith. But this is her house.

"Yes." I see her through the reflection of the mirror.

"Destiny, there is nothing I want more than for you to find love, happiness, and all other good stuff that goes with it. But, baby, I don't feel like we've seen the last of that man yet. And I don't want you so caught up in Mac that you miss it. Here, let me do it." Faith reaches for the comb and the spray bottled of water. She slowly starts detangling my bushy curls.

It all seems like the worst possible conundrum: Fear or love. Living a happy life or always looking over my shoulder, wondering when the combat boot of my past will kick me in the ass.

Faith adds a few drops of oil in her hand and rubs them together. She spreads it across the ends of my hair and starts braiding. I switch from chewing my lip to picking at my chipped black nail polish.

"Just promise me one thing."

I look up from my hand as Faith focuses on braiding. I cross my legs and adjust my head slightly to tilt as she progresses toward the base of my neck.

"Pay attention. Keep your eyes wide open. Think of nothing as a coincidence. And remember that man makes his living tracking people down."

A cold chill rushes through my body. But I'm tired of allowing Ryan and fear to dictate my life. Isn't that why I left? I'm out of options. The only way to get over my fear and Ryan is to leave them where they belong—in my past.

MY NEED FOR SPEED STARTED THE MOMENT MY FEET touched the ground. Mom says I ran before I walked. Always hurrying from one place to the other, from one stage to another, from one project to another. It's an attribute stuck to my personhood like gum stuck to the sole of a shoe.

At times it's uncomfortable and unsettling, but it's how I work, and I'm starting to believe it's too late to change it. I guess that's why I find solace in rebuilding cars. Restoration projects force patience, ordering parts, rebuilding part by part, screw by screw until the beauty emerges.

I sit in the dark of my temporary home—a modular home sitting on twenty acres. During the light of day, I can sit in this very spot and see the concrete slab for my home. But building takes time and patience. Patience I'm learning with age to embrace but not without a lot of moaning and groaning on my part because my inner self desires speed.

I want it now.

I close my eyes and see Destiny's hair floating in the wind. The faster I took us, the more I witnessed the sexy smile play at the corners of her sweet lips. I groan.

"Patience Mac."

Because I don't just want her, I want her now. And I should be ashamed for rushing things with Destiny, but I'm not.

Zero to one hundred is how I live my life. My need for speed translates into an all or nothing mentality, and I want all of her.

I nurse the brown liquor, hoping after a beautiful day with Destiny, hoping that it will keep the dreams away.

I've sought counseling through the VA and privately. But nothing stops the dreams.

I lift the drink to my mouth, and the clinging of the ice against glass brings back our last mission. My head drops back, trying to fight off the ringing of the explosion. The screams of the people. The blood splattered across my uniform. Holding my best friend as he died.

Tears trail down my face. I grab the neck of the bottle, pushing the glass aside, letting my grief consume me. I lift the bottle when a chime rings. I look toward the sound, and the light from my cellphone glows. I'll check it later.

I tilt the bottle to my mouth, and my phone chimes again. I lower the cognac, staring at my phone. I place the bottle on the end table and push to my feet. I sway a little then level my gaze on the singing device.

I take calculated steps until I have the phone in my hands. I turn the screen to me blinking as my eyes adjust to the brightness. Three messages from...Destiny Mitchell.

I unlock my phone and read the message. *Oh...sorry for the time.*

I retrace my steps sitting back in my chair. I back up and start with the first message. *I'm sure you're sleeping. But thanx.*

It took FOREVER to detangle my hair. Why didn't you

tell me I looked like a Treasure Troll?! I laugh. "A beautiful troll," I whisper as the desire for her pushes through the clouds of my regrets.

You're welcome. I text back. I reach for the bottle, and no matter how bad I want to keep the dreams of Kenneth's death at bay, I don't want to miss a single thought about Destiny or our day together. Instead of taking another drink, I let out the recliner, closing my eyes.

And instead of wishing the bad dreams away, I hope the pain I've endured gives me a pass this time. That I won't experience this feeling only to lose it. And I consider that maybe I've done something right in this life to bring Destiny to me.

CHAPTER ELEVEN

"Angel, pass me the wrench." I twist my arm, trying to find the right angle while keeping an ear on Destiny. I hear the sound of metal clanking against metal, then the swooshing of my tools from one side of the box to the other.

"Angel?" She's standing next to the car with her plaits back giving me an unobstructed view of her face.

"Thoughts of you chase away my demons. I figure you must be an angel." The crimson covers her face, and my heart glows.

"Mac, you flirt as well as you breathe." She rocks into her hip, wagging her finger.

"Maybe." I wink and chuckle.

"Here." She thrusts the wrench in my direction.

I lean back, surprised, and I smile at her gloomy face. "By golly, I think she's got it."

"Oh, hush." She chuckles, spinning around and walking back to her seat beside the car. I get a good look at her as she walks away. She drops to the old lawn chair, and the flowing material of her dress exposes more of her leg than I recall seeing before. Our eyes hold, and she pulls the fabric over her knee.

My eyes find hers. I smile pleased at the desire I see. But it doesn't override her sour mood.

I came out to work in the garage around four, and to my surprise, the woman of my dreams arrived shortly after five. Three hours early? Something is wrong with my angel.

Last night I only slept a few hours, but I didn't drink myself into a stupor, and instead of death waiting for me, I dreamt of crazy curly hair and my hazel-eyed beauty. There's something about Destiny. I'm enjoying having her around, and I can't decipher if it's timing or her or both.

Losing my best friend gives me a different perspective on life and what it means to have a future worth living. He didn't have a chance to do all the things we discussed our whole life, but I do. Even if some days I wished I could switch places because he had a wife and a child.

Last night, her text made me realize switching places with Kenneth would have meant forfeiting this moment. I would have never fixed her tire, spent the day in town and explored these new feelings she's churning inside of me.

So, I guess the best place to start is with moving forward. I have to stop letting the past overshadow my present starting with the blood bath that ended my military career.

I look over at her sitting in the chair. Destiny is playing with her plait, deep in thought. I've let her sit beside the car and pout for almost two hours. I shrug it off, figuring she'll level with me when she's ready. I tighten the bolt.

For a split second, I wonder if she's having second thoughts about us. Then the wrench slips from my hand. *When had she and I become us?*

I pick up the wrench, unable to identify the moment but sometime between fixing her flat, hiring, kissing her, and last night. And now I'm tied to a woman determined to move on from Madison Grove.

Can I convince her to stay?

The selfish man in me asks for the thousandth time. I'm not sure, but I damn sure plan to try. There's nothing like a small town when you're surrounded by family and friends and by love.

Love, dude, really? I freeze.

Instalove. Fate. Destiny.

I'm flawed, selfish, and I still see no reason not to make her mine. *Zero to one hundred.*

Maybe it's not love but intense like and extreme chemistry. Whatever it is, it's as natural as breathing and I'm ready to live fully with her beside me. Now to get her to agree to at least consider Madison Grove as an option.

"Try to turn it over again for me."

Destiny stands and sits behind the wheel. She turns it once, and I hear the 'Vette gurgle. Then she tries again, and the rumble of the engine fills the garage.

"Yeehaw!" I pump my fist in the air.

Destiny stands from inside the car with a silly smile on her face. I shrug, it's a McKenzie thing. Then I curl a finger in her direction. The humor in her dreamy eyes morphs into desire, and again she pleases me by walking in my direction. She doesn't stop until we're inches from each other.

I lower my head and brush my lips against hers. A sensual smile spreads across her face. Then I take my time and nibble on her sweet lips.

"Angel, your smile does something to me," I whisper across her lips, kissing here and there.

"And what's that?" She leans into me on her tiptoes as if she can't get enough, not caring that I'm filthy. I'll probably get grease all over her pretty dress.

"Keep pouting, and I'll make it my personal mission to show you." I step back, locking eyes with her. I yank the rag from my waistband and wipe the oil from my hands.

"Don't threaten me with a good time, Ethan McKenzie."

"It's not a threat, Angel." I slam the hood closed. "Let's turn a few corners."

Destiny's in the tattered passenger seat before I can round the car. I sit beside her. I glance over, dropping a hand on her exposed thigh. She leans over and kisses me before sitting back. This woman is good for me.

I press the accelerator a few times listening to the sound of the engine. Then I pull out of the garage and inch us down the dirt path to the old country road.

"Let's see what this baby can do."

Destiny lowers her shades. "Let's."

I shift the gear into first, and we burn off. Heading toward Madison Grove and passing town until there's nothing but open road. I push the 'Vette to eighty... ninety...then one hundred miles an hour. The fields swish past in green blurs, and I feel one step closer to honoring Kenneth's death.

We ride about twenty minutes, and I make my usual turnaround to check the car. I don't want her overheating. I turn off the road to a gravel spot with a little picnic table under an old oak tree.

I get out and lift the hood, peeking around for leaks,

smoke, or anything needing my attention. I pushed her hard, and she performed like a champ.

"Shit." I burn the side of my index finger.

"Be careful." Destiny's beside me, taking my hand. She examines it. "Hold on, let me get my first-aid kit."

I watch her retreating back. Curiosity makes me place one foot in front of the other until I can see her reaching inside the car for her pink backpack. I noticed it before because she's never without it. I didn't give it much thought, figured it was a purse. Then she returns with a little white box.

I watch her clean the burn and apply ointment. She's focused on the task, and I'm focused on her with one question banging around in my head. Who carries a first-aid kit? *And why?*

Okay, so that's two questions. Are these more pieces to the puzzle of her past?

"Destiny..." She glances up. "What happened yesterday?"

"Faith and I had a disagreement." She kisses my finger. "There, all better."

"Thank you." I kiss her neck, and she wiggles from my reach. "And?"

"She believes I'm moving too fast with you." She crosses her arms, leaning into her hip with a gentle rock.

This got my attention. I slam the hood closed.

I sit on the edge of the car and watch her as she resumes her pacing.

"She's worried that Ryan will return…" His name was Ryan. "And I told her I refused to be intimated by him any longer."

Destiny spins around and resumes her stance. I'll address the sister issue then Ryan.

"Do you believe Faith made the statements to hurt you?"

She looks away, "No."

"Then what harm will it do to consider her position?"

I don't want to be the source of their disagreement, but I also don't want to be the source of placing Destiny in danger. Faith is not an unreasonable person, and this is the second time I've heard about his potential to harm Destiny.

"Because it feels like he wins."

The words creeped out and wrapped their claws around my heart and from the pit of my soul, I claim her. She's mine, and it's time I fill in the details about this Ryan character because he's not worth her smiles or her happiness.

Destiny Mitchell doesn't have a clue, but she's wrapping me around her sweet little finger, and I can't stop it from happening any more than I can stop my heart from beating. I want to know more now, but she's already worked up. It's time I learned to pace myself.

"How about we grab some chow? I know Faith loves you and you love her. With that, this is repairable. First Faith and then we'll see about squaring away this thing with Ryan for good."

I reach out and circle my hands around her waist, pulling her close until she's standing between my outstretched legs. She relaxes in my arms, and I want nothing more than to keep her safe. Somewhere deep inside I question whether I'm the man for the mission. But I have to be if I want to keep her.

MAC PARKS IN FRONT OF MADDIE'S COUNTRY KITCHEN. He opens the door and helps me out of the Corvette. His hand rests on my lower back, and he guides us toward the diner. I glance up as his eyes sweep the area around us. He has a way of appearing relaxed, but his eyes give him away. He covers every inch of a room within seconds. I guess it's the soldier in him.

"Semper Fi, devil dog!" A man dressed in a uniform stops in front of us.

Mac smiles and they bump fists. "How long have you been back, devil dog?"

"It's my first day home."

"Nice."

I listen, but they're speaking in some kind of code. I looked across the street and see the lights of the boutique.

I touch Mac's arm and whisper, "I'll be right back."

He nods. "Remember, she loves you."

I know, and I'll take his advice. I look both ways before crossing Main Street. Part of me still can't believe I'm back. They cleaned up the downtown area since I left after graduation and the upgrades were family-friendly with the addition of a park and the entertainment complex. I make a mental note to check it out. Faith says there's a skating rink inside. The last time I went roller skating, I was still wearing a training bra.

I stop outside the shop and see Faith through the window, she's adding jewelry to a mannequin. She glances my way and waves. I wave back. Mac is right, this is repairable even if we have to agree to disagree.

I walk toward the boutique door, and the sight of a police cruiser pulling out of the parking lot sends a wave of anxiety through my body and my heart races in slow motion. The sound of a sluggish train floods my ears. I focus on breathing and getting inside the shop. I lower my head and increase my pace, trying not to draw attention to myself.

I yank the door open, welcoming the sound of the bells overhead and the coolness of the shop. I pushed the door closed and look back out the window. The cruiser passes the shop without the cop even looking my way.

I audibly exhale.

Chugga-chugga chugga-chugga.

Inhale. Exhale.

Chugga-chugga chugga-chugga.

I swallow with my eyes glued on the cruiser.

Ryan and his cop buddies changed my perception of law enforcement. I once thought of them as the cavalry, but now I toggled between skepticism and distrust. I know all cops aren't the same, but all the ones I've encountered did little to improve my views of them. They are merely men with silver and navy-blue badges that allow them to do as they damn well, please.

The fear turns my feet into concrete. I clutch the handle with my sweaty hands to keep from dropping to the floor. I can't move until the car is out of sight. And then my eyes lock with Mac's. He's still talking with the young man. I force a smile and wave. He nods, but I can see his eyes calculating the distance between us.

"What's that all about?" Faith says over my shoulder.

"Nothing important."

I walk into the boutique and observe the progress. Most of the boxes are gone, and the sections in the shop are clearly defined with a center aisle leading to the register. To the right are the teen, sales, and plus-size sections. On the left are seasonal and trendy, children's, and the last section isn't as apparent to me.

"What's that section?" I point to the far-left corner.

"Faith's Picks. I'll highlight hot items and my favorites. I don't consider myself trendy, but I like classic staple pieces. I plan to rotate them by theme and season."

I pull out my new cellphone and snap a few pictures of Faith standing next to the counter. I wouldn't consider my sister trendy either but elegant. Her keen eye for fashion shows.

I scroll through the pictures. "I love this one. I think it would be great to share in your newsletter." I turn my screen to her.

"What do you mean?" Faith asks with a puzzled expression on her face as she takes my phone.

"Well, you could select an item or color and style it. Then we'd post that picture and your thoughts on your social media accounts and in your email newsletter. That will encourage people to visit and share. And all of it means more potential customers for the boutique."

Faith's eyes glow with excitement. "You're *really* good at this."

"Thank you." Maybe one day I can have my own business too. "I came to apologize about last night." I step closer and grab Faith's hands. "You're my sister, and I love you. I know you're concerned for me. I guess I'm just adjusting to it all. Having people around that care for me is different."

Faith nods and pulls me to her. We hug, and I realize I've missed so much running from city to city. No more, I decide. Thanks to Faith, I have a family again.

The chime of the bells brings our mushy moment to an end. I brush away my tears, and Faith does the same, an awkward giggle passes between us as Mac makes his way down the aisle in our direction.

I turn gladly, taking in the sight.

CHAPTER TWELVE

"FAITH, LOOK AT THIS PLACE." I HUG FAITH AND KISS HER forehead. "Has Chris stopped by?" I release Faith and reach for Destiny's hand. Her lack of hesitation pleases me, and I place a kiss on the back of her hand.

"Yes." Her response is tight.

"When will you two stop dancing around each other?" I scrub my free hand down my face.

"Christopher wants a casual relationship. I deserve a commitment." Faith shrugs and turns her face from me, but I saw the hurt in her eyes. "Can you give me a hand with a display cabinet?"

"You get the pizza and point me in the direction of the box," I tease, trying to lighten the mood. She gives me a quick hug and heads toward the back office.

I exchange glances with Destiny then turn to watch Faith walk away. I need to talk to my brother.

"What was all that devil dog talk about?" Destiny captures my attention, placing a hand on my chest.

"It's a Marine thing." I wrap an arm around her waist and kiss the side of her neck.

"Oh, really…"

"Yes, really…" I brush a kiss on her soft lips, wanting to sample her sweetness, but Destiny surprises me when she tilts her head and deepens the kiss.

A chime rings but the smile lingering on Destiny's face makes me want another kiss until I hear, "Get a room."

"Look at little Destiny," Chris speaks in his baby voice, always the jokester, about everything except his money.

"Ha, haha." She walks over and hugs Chris. "How are you?"

"I'm good. Welcome home." He growls, pretending to squeeze her tight and Destiny giggles. "Mac said you were back and working at the shop. I saw his new website. You and I need to talk because I'd love an upgrade for my company site."

I'm proud of her. Maybe getting more business will help her get back on her feet and help make staying more appealing. The Reese & Sons website is updated with a fresh, modern design. Then she surprised us by adding details about the repair shop and Mac's Muscle

Cars. She accomplished this in a week. I can only imagine what we'll do with more time.

"I'd love to. Can you give me a couple of weeks? I want to get the auto consignment and storage facility integrated with the client portal. That should keep this guy and Brittany from strangling each other."

I doubt it would solve the Brittany dilemma, especially after her rotten attitude toward Destiny. It sealed the decision to release her in my eyes. Her gum popping and rude behavior are unbearable.

"That'll work. So that means you're sticking around?" Chris asks.

I tense, watching the exchange between them. This is the question of the hour. Chris' direct questioning could rival the best attorney. It's what makes him an esteemed businessman. He's straightforward and goals oriented, which makes his situation with Faith out of character. But I know my brother—the level gaze zeroed in on Destiny tells me he's meddling. I wait ready to hear her response.

"Look at who we have here." Faith returns, pushing a large box on a dolly.

"Hello, gorgeous." Chris turns on his mega-watt smile, redirecting his attention to Faith.

The abrupt shift in the topic seems to throw Destiny for a loop too, as her eyes dart between the two. I wrap my hands around Destiny, pulling her out of the crossfire. I stop once her back is against my chest. She'll have a better view from this angle.

"Don't 'Hey gorgeous' me." Faith stops crossing her arms, and leans into her hip just like Destiny—it must be a sister thing. "We are not open to the public until next week."

"You don't say." Chris steps closer to Faith.

"I didn't stutter."

"Well, that's not what you said last night."

Destiny's soft gasp mirrors my shock. Faith doesn't appear disturbed as she takes a step closer to Chris. These two are better than a pay-per-view boxing match.

"Apparently you have selective hearing. I told you to stay on your side of the street, and I'll stay on mine." She points the directions out, making it clear to all of us.

Chris takes another step, and his voice drops to a lethal tenor. "And I told *you*, make me."

Destiny's breathing increases. Her chest rises and falls, and I feel her muscles flex to move. I whisper in her ear, "Don't."

I know she wants to jump in, but her sister is a big girl, and she needs to tell Chris to man up or step off. And I will support Faith in doing so.

"Don't test me, Christopher McKenzie." Seeps out so low I almost miss it.

Chris steps back and his deal-closing smile doesn't reach his eyes. "Have it your way, Cupcake. You'll need me, and when you do, you know where to find me. I'll be on *my* side of the street."

I know Chris better than any person on the planet. The throb in his jaw and the intensity in his eyes as he storms out of the boutique spells war. I hope Faith knows what she's doing.

———

MAC LEADS US TO THE WATERSIDE PARK BEHIND THE downtown area created beside a man-made reservoir. We select a picnic table close to the water.

"What was that all about?" I straddle the bench removing our to-go containers. We went to Maddie's Country Kitchen to pick up our *chow* and give Faith some time alone.

"That was Faith finally standing up for herself."

"I could learn a thing or two from my big sister." I pass Mac his dinner first with a handful of napkins before sitting.

"Thanks, in what way?"

I think about his question. I shrug, "Every way."

"Explain." Mac sits across from me and opens the Styrofoam container.

"Well for starters, she has her life together. She has a home and a business, she's independent."

"Those are things I believe you're very capable of obtaining if you want them. You're a talented designer. I bet you could get a lot of business here in Madison Grove once they see the work you've done for us and then Chris. And he has business contacts across the state. But is that what you want?" He pops a fry in his mouth then removes a Texas-size cheeseburger. I shake my head stunned by the size, it's enormous.

"I honestly don't know. It's all happening so fast. I guess I'll have to take it one day at a time because I never thought starting my own business was an option. I've been too busy trying to survive."

Granted, I've loved working on Mac's website. It's been more extensive than Faith's site because Reese & Sons is much more than junk. I've found it challenging and fun. Like the client portal, it's something I learned in school, but now I get to actually build a payment system.

I pop a hot fry in my mouth, and it burns going down, but it's so tasty, with just enough seasoning and not too much salt. I search around Mac's area and snatch one of his ketchup packets.

"Hey! Get your own." He laughs.

I laugh with him then we dig in. We talk about

nothing and everything until we eat in comfortable silence. This is different. It seems unreasonable to draw comparisons, but it's hard not to.

Is this what peace feels like? To not constantly live in fear. To sit with an amazing man eating a big ass greasy burger until I'm stuffed. To laugh until I cry. To ride with the top down not caring about my hair. To have a job and Faith and Mr. Reese and Chris and Mac and even Brittany with her damn gum.

I'm living for the first time in my life, and it feels good. And I'll gladly take it. Again, and again and again. I've had eight days of freedom, and I pray I never take it for granted.

Then I stop to think about Mac's question. What do I want? *What do I want?*

I lean into the weather-worn bench until my chin rests in the palm of my hand. The sound of laughter floats through the air and stirs around me. I see the source. A woman with a small child feeding the ducks near the lake. The woman tries to slow him down to actually feed the ducks, but he seems focused on chasing them. The more they run, the faster his little feet take him, the louder his laughter gets.

Can I have that? I bite back tears. Can I be so bold as to ask this life that dealt me a fucked-up hand to give me laughter and peace? I lost my mother to drugs. I never knew my father. My grandmother died. I lost my sisters to the system. I've had more black eyes, bruised ribs, and busted lips than I can count. Now at twenty-nine, dare I ask for joy? And maybe...just maybe real love?

"What are you thinking over there?" Mac asks. His eyes always feel like a warm blanket, and unlike the men before him, I know he cares about my response.

"I'm thinking about your question. I guess I've been running for so long that I stopped thinking about what I want. The immediate demands seem to overshadow thought of my future."

"So...what'll it be, Jelly Bean?" I can't contain my smile.

Hearing the nickname is always a dig, but it makes me think of happier times and eating jelly beans until I got sick. All because I wanted to prove to my sisters that I knew all the flavors by heart. Will I ever be that fearless girl again? It's time I find out.

"I want to be happy." Mac nods and I stare deep in his eyes, and I swear the man is casting a spell over me. "Is that too much to ask?"

"Not at all. Eat, Angel, and we'll work out the details later."

I nod, placing my trust in Mac, and a part of me feels like he's doing the same. Something is different between us today. It's like he and I are *we*. Hum.

I take a big bite of my burger and groan. "Ohhh, this is delicious!"

"Told you. Don't sleep on Maddie's and their meatloaf is better than Mom's." He uses a napkin to wipe the grease I feel on the side of my mouth. "Are you happy now?"

"I am, more than I thought possible." I search the depths of his eyes, and I feel butterflies. I can't recall a time in my adult life when I've been truly happy. Mac has a lot to do with it and not just his amazing kisses but the man. It makes me consider all the ways he and Ryan differ.

"So how about we do this?" Mac reaches for my hand. "Let's explore this season of life together. You can continue at the shop. The office is yours to manage our needs and bring on other clients if you'd like. Just say you'll stay."

"I'll agree under one condition," I say with authority, and his grip tightens. This is my opportunity to start over. I'd be a fool to walk away. "You must seal the deal with a kiss."

"Yes, ma'am."

The passion in Mac's eyes ignites as he tosses the napkin aside and walks around the table. He pulls me to my feet, cupping my head. Our kiss starts as a slow burn and heats up. His lips work mine, and I can't get close enough. But I try when I wrap my arms around his neck. I want more of him as heat from my desire flows through my veins. I'm ready for whatever Mac has in store.

"So, I guess this means I'm your girlfriend?"

"Yeah, that or my ole' lady, your pick."

I throw my head back, laughing. "I guess ole lady it is."

CHAPTER THIRTEEN

THE RIDE BACK TO THE SHOP IS DREAMY. I CAN'T BELIEVE Mac wants a relationship with me. *What about Ryan?*

The thought is the dark cloud threatening to rain on an otherwise perfect day. Thoughts of Ryan made the dreamy moment feel more like a cloudy haze, and I looked over at Mac. Men like him don't usually pick women like me. He comes from a good family, he served in the military. He is gentle and kind, and patient. Nothing like any man I've dated or known. What do I have to offer him?

"We're here."

The car stops in front of the shop. I blink out of the wicked haze of my thoughts.

"What is it?" He reaches for my hand.

"I'm just tired, I think."

"I can take you home." He searches for something in

my eyes. I grab my backpack from the floorboard to keep him from seeing the truth, that I'm ready, but I'm scared. All of my relationships start out good. They didn't roll up and introduce themselves as aggressive, manipulative, or abusive. No, it was sweet talk, long walks then—

Brittany knocks on Mac's window, and I welcome the interruption. I use the break to get out of the car. I need to retreat to my office and work. I have less than an hour before Faith is scheduled to pick me up.

"Destiny, where are you—"

"I'll see you inside."

I use long strides to put space between us. I pull open the door, and the smell of something familiar assaults my nose. The eerie feeling of that dark cloud moves closer. I clutch my backpack to my chest, spinning around the front service area.

The boxes, old parts, and misplaced knick-knacks are gone. It's bright and open, leading to the front counter.

"What is that smell?" I sniff, lifting my nose in the air. Mr. Reese stands behind the counter with an oil-covered part nestled in his hand.

"Some fool came in smoking a cigar." He shakes his head as if in disbelief then scrubs an oil-stained rag along the silver part. "He didn't see the sign." He uses the rag-filled hand to point to the sign over my shoulder.

I recognize the scent. My greatest complaint with Ryan and his friends was the constant smoking in the house. The smell always lingered long after they stumbled out into the night. No matter how often I complained, no one seemed to care about how it caused my asthma to act up.

"How did they know about it?" Mac entered the shop, talking with Brittany, and I remember my destination is my office, not here. I walk around the counter and beeline to my office. I can feel Mac's eyes on me, but I refused to look back.

I enter my office, locking the door behind me. I rest against the closed door with my eyes shut. The cool wood door is a direct contrast to my increased body temperature. Have I made a mistake?

Knock knock. The soft knock makes me jump. I glance over my shoulder.

"What is it?"

I can't respond. What should I tell him? That I'm spooked again. That I don't know whether I can trust my own judgment.

"Open the door—let's talk," he whispers. His energy permeates through the door, and I want to open it, but I can't.

"I just need a moment. Alone." I exhale.

Mac grips the doorknob, turning it rapidly from side

to side. He tries again, and I pull out my cellphone to text Faith to pick me up.

"Did I do something?"

I shake my head but remain silent. We stand in a silent standoff with the door between us. I breathe rapidly in and out of my mouth.

Mac shakes the handle again, and I jump, remembering the night I left Ryan. I trembled in fear as he kicked the door and yelled obscenities. The way Ryan's anger vibrated off the walls of my immaculate prison.

"Fine." It's not loud, but I hear it.

I don't know how much time passes as I stand against the door with my backpack crushed to my chest. Then a knock startles me.

A sense of urgency floods my body. That smell. I know that smell. Maybe it's a sign that I'm making a mistake. Trusting Mac? Staying in Madison Grove?

Parts of me feels like returning to Ryan is easier than waiting, wondering when he will turn up. Because he always manages to find me. It wasn't a matter of if but when.

And Mac...I turn to the door. Only the sound of my breathing fills the room. He left. Maybe I've pushed him away too. A single tear falls from my eye. I'm confused and mixed up and have no idea what to do next.

Should I run to Mac and apologize, or should I take

this as a sign? He could do better and if he really wanted to be with me then somewhere in him is a monster just like the others.

My mind runs like the coding I love. The reliability of the combinations. The predictability of the outcome. I'd be the piece of code that crashes the whole damn program.

My phone rings. It's Faith. "Yeah."

"I'm here." Her voice is distant, and I hear the fall breeze.

"Here, I come," I huff out.

I disconnect the call, stopping to listen. I've learned to be one with the objects around me, to observe when life is about to throw another unexpected virus. I look around my office, committing my first office to memory. There's nothing special, really. It's the pieces that make me want to capture it for safekeeping.

An old office desk, a blue cloth chair on wheels, a silver and black guest chair half facing the desk and half facing the wall. It doesn't take much to see Mac lounging in the chair as he's done daily since I started working here. But my work here is almost complete. The final element is the payment portal, and I can finish the coding from Faith's place. There's no real reason to come back to Reese & Sons except Mac.

The thought of walking away from him makes my chest tighten as my heart protests—in a silent, violent groan. I crush the floral fabric of my dress above my heart in a fist, willing it to stop.

Please stop.

My heart's betrayed me enough times for me to disregard its interference. But it's never...never felt like this.

I can't think with the scent lingering in the distance, a scent my instincts attribute to Ryan. I know it's not real, Ryan's not here. But I can't think when all I want is to feel the comfort of Mac's presence or the feel of his lips against mine. I don't have the guts to tell him I'm not sure I fit into this picture. Not when the hint of tobacco brings Faith's words back like a haunting truth. I haven't seen the last of that man. Leaving is best.

I walk to the door and twist the handle. I stick my head out, sweeping the hall with a glance from one end to the other. There's no Mac. I step out and turn out the lights, closing the door behind me. I walk past the front counter where Brittany is closing out the register. She shifts from counting out the bills to pushing around the coins.

"I'll see you tomorrow." My pitiful attempt at sounding cheerful isn't missed by moody Brittany. She rolls her eyes and scribbles a number on a piece of receipt paper. Her attitude pitted against my already foul mood makes for a thick tension in the air.

I look over Brittany's shoulder, and the light in Mr.

Reese's office is out, which means the two of us are alone.

"What did I ever do to you?" I ask.

"I don't like you." Brittany slams the drawer closed. "Mac might be sniffing all behind you, but I bet you'll be gone before the holidays."

"Whatever." I continue to the door. She's right, but I won't give her the satisfaction of knowing it.

"Just do us all a favor and carry your ass back to where you came from."

I push the door open and head to Faith's old Camry, not looking back. I'll have Madison Grove in my rearview mirror the moment I finish the portal and collect the remainder of my pay. I've saved enough money to get to my next stop.

The way I figure it. I can finish everything by the end of the week, which means I could probably squeeze in Chris' website design too. That would give me enough money to put more distance between myself and Texas. Maybe I'll try my luck in California.

I sit in the car. I'll stay for Faith's opening as promised and leave Sunday. I ignore the aching throb in my chest as I fasten my seatbelt. I have five days left in Madison Grove.

THE FRUSTRATION OF DESTINY'S HOT AND COLD treatment sends me out of the shop. The gravel beneath my feet carries me closer to my sanctuary and away from *her*. This woman is trying to drive me mad. One minute we're perfect and the next we're strangers with an invisible line drawn in the sand. Will she ever *really* let me in?

I can't profess to understand women or know much about relationships. They've never been a priority, not when I spent most of my military career overseas. I guess I figured when I found her—whoever she is—it would flow. Wrong. Asking Destiny to be my lady means something to me only to have her shut me out.

I enter the office door to keep the garage door closed. I need some privacy. I flick on the light, emptying the contents from my pockets onto the desk. Brittany brought me a card for potential buyers. They came around asking about Mac's Muscle Cars. I smile. It begins. I haven't officially opened my doors, and people are already interested in my cars. Destiny's website is working.

Destiny...

I pull my shirt off, tossing it in the chair. I need a work shirt. I search the bottom drawer for something old because I'm ready to get dirty. Then a thought comes to mind. I check the time and reach for my cellphone.

"Yo, KJ." I push the speaker button and throw on my shirt.

"Hey, Uncle Mac."

He's in junior high now and asked us to stop calling him Little Kenny. *Man, is he Kenneth's son.* I smile. Kathryn was shocked into silence. It's official, our little man is growing up.

I sit back in the chair, listening as he updates me on his week. "I got a 'Vette and some pizza at the garage. Want to hang with me tonight?"

"Let me ask Mom."

I wait, dropping my keys and change back into my pocket. Little Kenny loves cars just like his father. Agreeing to be his godfather gives me more than I could ever give him. And helping Kathryn raise him feels like having my childhood all over again, except this time I'm only half as stupid. I laugh because Kenneth, Chris, and I were reckless and an absolute handful for our parents.

I pick up the business card, noticing the Dallas area code.

"Uncle Mac?"

"Yeah." I put the card aside.

"Mom said yes, since I've finished my homework. But you have to have me back by ten."

"Cool. I'm on my way."

I disconnect the call standing. I consider taking the 'Vette again, but I head to my truck instead. I'm not ready to see another passenger in the seat beside me. I stop and double back and grab the business card. Let me call now.

I pick up the receiver to the desk phone. I still have a landline out here. It seems outdated and an unnecessary expense, but it serves us well when the weather gets bad or when there's a poor cellphone reception. I dial the number sitting on the edge of the desk.

The phone rings and I hear a generic voicemail message. "This is Ethan McKenzie with Mac's Muscle Cars leaving a message for Ryan Brenton. You can reach me at ..." I leave the number to my garage and the website address. It feels good to have my first potential buyer.

I need to get moving since it's a school night. I reach for the door, determined to set ,aside Destiny and her issues.

I climb into the cabin of my truck, making my way to the old country road. Thoughts of her soft skin, her flowing hair in the wind, and the way it feels to hold her in my arms assault me. I stop at the edge of our driveway. I want her in every way. But I won't force it, and apparently, she doesn't want me. Not like I want her.

It's only been a fucking week Mac. But what is time, really?

I've lost more in seconds than I've gained in years.

Putting feelings on a timeline ranks close to waiting to marry the one you love. You either do, or you don't—there's no in-between for me.

I guess my zero to one hundred ways are kicking me in the ass again. I thought I could be patient. However, Destiny locking me out of her office shows me I've rushed it. I'll back off.

I pull out to the old road and head to town. I haven't seen Little Kenny in a couple of weeks. He needed time to adjust to the new school year. I turn on the music and cover the distance within minutes. Kathryn stayed in Madison Grove after Kenneth's death, which allows me to help her the way Kenneth wanted.

I stop in front of their single-story home, and Little Kenny is out the door before the wheels on my truck stop.

"What up?" We dab fists after he climbs in the truck.

"Nothing much. Did you grow another five inches?"

He laughs. "Nah, but Mom said I've already outgrown my new school clothes."

"We'll see about getting you some new ones."

"Yes, sir."

"Hey, Kat! How's the business going?" I call out to her on the porch, and she walks over.

"I'm blessed. We have a waiting list for newborns, and I'm almost at 90% enrollment." She opened a daycare business over by the community center this time last year.

"Nice." I lean back into the door. "How's it feel?"

"Unreal. I can't believe I'm actually doing it. But I am." She smiles and steps back to the curb. "I'll let you guys go. Oh, Chris told me about your new website. Can your girl get the hookup?"

"I'll see what I can do."

"All right. You can give her my cellphone number. I'd love to get something as soon as possible. I hate relying on Facebook."

"No doubt. I'll give it to her tomorrow."

"All right, I'll see you later, son. Bye, Mac." She heads into the house.

"Let's stop and get the pizza."

"Bet." He puts on his seatbelt, slouching back in the seat.

Kenneth and I were the original ebony and ivory. Our folks are friends, and we remained friends our entire lives. We got plenty of chicks when we told them we were brothers—with the same mom but different dads. And the girls bought it even though we looked nothing alike. I still laugh at our crazy antics.

Little Kenny and I now get the same looks when people see us together, and they hear him calling me Uncle Mac. But the people around Madison Grove see it as a sequel because Little Kenny is Kenneth's clone.

We head to town and talk about sports and girls, like a true teenage boy would. I park outside the pizzeria, pausing to look down at Faith's Boutique. I see the car parked out front. I think about Destiny. Her smile flutters across my mind, but I push it out. We could have something special. But for now, I'll give her some space.

CHAPTER FOURTEEN

Dinner is uneventful. I sit across the table from Faith with a pizza box between us. The walls around us are covered with pictures. How did Faith manage to get our old childhood pictures? It makes her place feel like home.

"I think I've had more pizza this week than I've had in my entire life." Faith pushes the plate away from her.

My sister is tired, it's written on her beautiful face. We sort of figured as kids that our fathers are different, but Granny wasn't certain. I take another bite of the rubbery cheese pizza. It's easier to chew than talk about my plans and my uncertainty. Should I stay or leave? Should I trust that this place is where I belong? Should I rely on knowledge of Ryan Brenton? All the choices are overwhelming, but not more than the thought of leaving Mac.

"Destiny, what's going on with you? You're awful quiet."

I shrug in a noncommittal way and focus on the paper plate. "Nothing really. I'm about finished with Mac's site. It turned out well. I think he got his first car inquiry today."

That brings a smile to my face.

I pursued my college degree online and fell in love with coding. I guess Ryan's desire to keep me under his control helped me find a job I'm passionate about and I finished near the top of my class. I didn't get to walk, but I have my college degree folded in the back of my journal. It reminds me that I can do anything I put my mind to.

I guess this is another one of those moments to fold away and help me see myself a little clearer. I did well in school, but Faith and Mac are my first real clients. Knowing my designs are contributing to growth of their businesses makes me think about my conversation with Mac. Maybe finding a job isn't the solution but finding more clients.

"That's great. I'm proud of you." Faith beams, squeezing my hand. "And your relationship with Mac, how's that going?"

I see his face, his eyes, his smile when I hear his name. The ache is as intense as before. I shut Mac out. I take another bite of the pizza, and I can't taste it. But I don't want to tell her how I'm trying to shut Mac out of my heart, so instead, I tell Faith about the cigar smell and locking myself in the office.

"I'm sure you'll have times when old memories will challenge your new life. I guess that's what makes the unknown such a challenge." She bends her legs, bringing them to her chest. "What are you going to do?"

"I have to leave after your opening. It's like I feel Ryan is close and I can't let him find me." Her concerned eyes find mine, and I can't let her tears deter me. "That was my original plan, Faith. This is just a pit stop to somewhere far away."

"And go where?"

I see the slight rock, a habit she's done since we were kids. Funny how so much has changed, yet so much remains locked in the fiber of our being. While I run, Faith internalizes.

"Maybe the Bay Area in California." This afternoon I combed through my journal, and the details about the Bay Area or the San Francisco area seem like a possible pairing with my skills, plus is far from here. But the thought of it is overwhelming. I need to search for a job and a place to stay. I figure I can cover my travel and about a month of living expenses. But if I sign Chris on as a client and finish his site, that should float me for another month or two.

"Why do you have to go all the way to California?

You have plenty of leads here, and you could always look for clients in Houston or Dallas."

"I think it's better if I put as much distance between myself and Dallas as possible. Besides, I don't want him showing up here."

I stand, unable to contain my anxious energy. I toss our paper plates into the empty cardboard box. I want nothing to do with Dallas. I can't risk crossing paths with Ryan. I walk into the kitchen and place the box on top of the closed garbage can.

"Destiny, running isn't the answer."

I gasp, turning to face her. "Running got me here, and I'm away from him. I'm not going back."

"I'm not saying go back. I'm saying stay here. You can live here. I have plenty of room. I can even create a little office space for you at the shop. I... can't lose you again." The last part is a whisper.

"Faith, you're not losing me. I just don't know." I can't imagine seeing Mac around and not spending time with him or running into his arms.

"Can you promise me one itty-bitty teenie-weenie thing?" The way she pinches her fingers together less than an inch apart mixed with the silly grin on her face make me walk back to the table and drop into the chair.

"Maybe."

"Promise you'll think about it. I know it might be selfish, but I want you here. And maybe, just maybe we can find Hope. And we…" Her voice breaks. She brushes away her tears with a sweeping motion. "I'd like to have our family again."

Faith's a protector, she's confident, she's a take-charge type of woman. She's my sister but really, more of a mother than our mother ever was. It probably has a lot to do with her being the eldest.

"I can't lose you again," she whispers. "I just can't. Once was more than my heart could bear."

"And you won't." I reach for Faith, and we hold each other in the middle of the dining room. My arms wrap around Faith's waist, and she rubs soothing circles on my back.

The foster care system managed to sever the one thing Granny struggled to maintain—our sisterhood. She was a single mother who lost both of her children. Her son was killed in the Persian Gulf War and her daughter, our mother, Patricia, was lost to men, drugs, and ultimately AIDS.

Granny took custody of us when Mom went to prison, and all seemed well until she suffered a heart attack. That disrupted our lives again, and it shifted our family dynamics because we didn't have any family members willing to care for us, and so we were separated.

Faith and I found each other in the last six months, thanks to social media. Apparently, she'd been looking for us and found me.

We started messaging each other, then emailing and sharing pictures, until finally, we started talking daily by phone and video calls. Something told me to keep it all to myself. And she had.

Madison Grove and Faith are secrets I wanted Ryan to know nothing about, and I'll do anything to protect my sister. *What if we can find Hope?*

The thought of having both of my sisters is enough for me to summon the courage needed to stand up to whatever is heading my way. I squeeze Faith tighter. But can I stand up to Ryan? And what about Mac? I'll have to think it over.

"So, you'll stay?" Faith mumbles against my chest.

"Yes, I'll stay." *For now.*

CHAPTER FIFTEEN

I stumble to the door. I'm hungover and tired of the constant ringing of the damn doorbell. I pull it open and step back as Mike forces himself inside. He turns his squinted eyes in my direction.

"Man, what the hell is wrong with you? This place is a mess. And why aren't you answering your phone?" Mike removes his shades standing in the middle of the living room.

I look around. The once spotless room is covered in takeout boxes. I have dirty clothes thrown on the loveseat and my blanket on the couch. I've taken to sleeping in the living room because I didn't want to sleep in the bedroom until Destiny returns. It just isn't the same. This house feels so empty.

I walk to the couch and gather my blankets and

tossed them to the floor, making room for him to sit down. I slump to the sofa, and he joins me.

"We have work to do, and you're about to lose your job sitting in here sulking over a woman."

"I thought she'd be back by now. But I can't find her." My words sound slurred at ten in the morning. The bottle's been my companion while I search and wait for her return. I rub my hand over my face and back through my dirty hair. I can't remember the last time I took a shower.

"Did you hear back from the car dealer?"

I shake my head, although I have no clue. My phone is somewhere, probably dead. I need to find it and plug it into the charger.

"I got a call from my contact about Destiny's computer."

A lead. I sit up and freeze, gripping my spinning head. Now, I can get Dez back.

"But I'm not giving you shit until you get yourself together." Mike stands up.

"What do you mean you're not giving it to me?" The anger brewing in my gut is burning off the haze of the alcohol. Mike knows more about Destiny, and I'm going to get it.

"You heard me. Look at you!" Mike thrusts his hand at me.

"I don't need your fucking advice." All I need is Destiny.

"What you need is a fucking housekeeper or a babysitter. Wash your ass and clean this fuckin' place up." Mike motions to the room. "You spend a million dollars on this house to treat it like trash. I guess that's some rich people shit."

"Kiss my ass. Give it to me!"

"No."

I lunge at Mike ready to take my aggression out on somebody anybody. It's been almost a month. Maybe she's gone for good this time, and the thought of it all makes me want to rip Mike's head off just to relieve the anger of it all. *How dare she?*

Mike steps to the side, and I don't pivot fast enough. I go tumbling to the floor. I glance back over my shoulder and he's laughing. I use the arm of the recliner to get back up.

"You look mad. Are you mad, Ryan?" he taunts me.

I slowly turn around with my eyes trained on Mike. I pull my hands up to a fighter stance. I shuffle forward and swing, connecting with Mike's jaw. "Give it to me."

"Make me." Mike returns the blow sending him stumbling back against the wall. "I ain't *giving* you shit. You let that bitch run all over you."

I swing. He's about to have a knuckle sandwich for

breakfast. That will teach him a thing or two about taunting me. "How'd that shit feel?"

Mike's head whips to the side, and he comes back with a jab in my gut. I fold over his fist as he rearranges my organs. I uppercut, connecting under his chin. The force of my movement sends him back. He lands on the floor with a loud thud.

I feel more alive than I have in weeks. My fighting is instinctual after years of kickboxing. But I take my eyes off him for a second, and Mike sweeps a leg beneath me. I slam flat on my back.

Mike pins me to the ground and punches me in the face. "That's for my sore jaw." He strikes me again. "That's for daring to hit my pretty face." He climbs back then stands over me. "Clean up, sober up. Here." He tosses a detox drink at me. "Flush that shit out of your system. I'll be back in two days."

Mike storms out.

I grab the bottle of detox. We use it to clean our piss before a mandatory drug test. I open the bottle and take a drink. The citrus taste will pair well with tequila. I stagger to the kitchen and search for a clean glass but have to settle for an old fast food cup.

Mike can kiss my ass. I pour the detox and add the tequila until the concoction brushes the brim of the cup. I'll flush the drugs from my system and finally get my Destiny home.

CHAPTER SIXTEEN

DESTINY ARRIVES AT THE SHOP EARLY, AS USUAL. THE notification chimes on my cellphone telling me the alarm system was disarmed. I open the upgraded security app.

Today, I'm heading into Houston to look at a few more cars. The website is working, and I need to scout for more inventory. Knowing Destiny arrives early and stays late gives me a little wiggle room to handle other matters outside the shop. It also gives me time away from *her*.

I wrap a hand around my first cup of coffee with a trained eye on Destiny as she makes her way through the front area of the shop. She surprised me when she asked to continue using the office in exchange for ongoing maintenance and updates of our website at no charge. I agreed for my own selfish reason. I still want her near.

I openly assess her through the security cameras. She's beautiful with her hair braided in two plaits. Her ankle-length dress is paired with a matching cardigan. The more she hangs around, the more I'm compelled to put her ex-boyfriend behind us. Why should I pay for his mistakes? All I want is to love her.

I take a drink of my warm coffee, wondering how I plan to handle this situation. She stops at the front counter to turn on the computer then heads to her office. I switch angles the moment she slips out of her office and heads to the break room.

The hurricane warnings last week delayed Faith's opening, the schools remained closed, and Little Kenny stayed over at my place. Together we made some significant progress on the 'Vette and unbeknownst to him, his birthday gift arrived yesterday.

He's turning sixteen. I found him a 1970 Ford Mustang—his father's favorite car. It's in horrible condition, and I got it for a steal. I can see the beauty beneath the weather-worn exterior. The seller almost paid me to have it towed off his property. It took everything in me not to whoop.

Little Kenny loves Ford Mustangs. He naturally gravitates to them when we go out scouting cars. I know this will make a lasting impact on him. So, I got

Kathryn's approval to hang out with him for the next couple of weeks to fix it up for the big day. I wish Kenneth could see him.

Kenneth used to fix cars and talk about starting a custom shop after the military. Time wasn't on our side. Now, I'm fixing cars with his teenage son. Who knew Kenneth's life would end on foreign soil, and he wouldn't survive to see his only son grow up?

It's a humbling thought. It was a thought that taught me the reality of life and death. And I've tried to live my life fully because my best friend's was cut short. I guess that's what has me thinking about Destiny. I don't want to make the mistake of deciding to repair our relationship later. Because later isn't promised.

Dad arrives and stops to talk with Destiny. He says something, and she throws her head back, laughing. Dad slaps his knee as joy covers his face. I tap the screen of my phone to hear their conversation.

"Those jokers ran for their lives with that dog hot on their heels." Dad says, comically walking to the front area.

"Did the dog catch them?" Destiny asks, leaning against the counter.

"You'll have to wait and see." Dad winks and lowers to his stool with a slight bend of his knees. I see the toll of time and age on his body as he moves slower, more deliberate. Destiny faces Dad, turning her back to me.

I've heard this story and wondered what caused Dad to tell it to her.

"They run up the drive until they reached the front of the side entrance out there." He points to the left. "That dog had to be a good seventy pounds," his hands open wide as if he holds a giant beach ball, "and Mac was nothing but skin and bones, a buck ten soaking wet." He chuckles.

"Papa Mac stop teasing." She counters with a smile in her voice. Dad insisted she stop calling him Mr. Reese and told her he'd only answer to Papa Mac. Which I think is more flirting because Brittany calls him Mr. Reese every day.

"Mac stopped at the entrance there and grabbed a pipe. Kenneth ran up the hood of a car and was screaming for him to run faster. But Mac spun and faced the dog with the metal pipe in his hands." He shakes his head. "I still don't know what possessed that boy to stop running. I could see him from my office window. His little face was tight.

"By this point, that dog knew Mac was scared of him. He'd chased them home for months. I kept asking why he walked past the Cleveland place, and he said, 'I don't want to be scared anymore.'"

"So, what did Mac do?" She moves across the room and sits across from Dad, her face full of curiosity. I brush my finger over the screen.

"You are an impatient one, aren't you?" They laugh. "Mac stood between the dog and Kenneth and stared that dog down. You should have seen him. He squared his shoulders, and I saw a fire in that boy's eyes.

"The dog skidded to a halt. A cloud of dust blocked my view. Then all I heard was the thunder of Mac's voice. 'Come on, you wanna bite me? I dare you.'"

"What!"

"The birds stopped chirping. The world stopped spinning on its axis. Mac and that dog had a face-off." His hands swept open as if cleaning the slate. I lean forward. Oh, Dad's got her eating out of his hands. She's barely in her chair.

"What happened?"

"Remind me to never tell you another story." He smiles.

"You keep threatening me, and I'll stop making your coffee. I'll leave it for Mac or Brittany."

I fold over laughing. Neither I nor Brittany brew coffee to Dad's standards.

"And you're feisty, I see why my son likes you." He smiles, showing all of his white teeth.

Dad still has all of his teeth, and Mom loves to boast about it. I need to talk to him about flirting with my ole lady, I chuckle.

"You wouldn't do that to me, would you?" Dad covers his heart.

"You know I won't. But finish the story."

He nods. "The dog took a step forward, and I thought Mac would start running again, but instead, he took a step forward too."

Destiny gasps but doesn't interrupt.

"I knew, at that moment, that my son was fearless." The sound drops out. I push the volume button, but it's at the maximum level. "They stood for about thirty seconds. It felt like an hour as I watched from the window. And suddenly the dog backed up and left."

Destiny lets out a loud breath. "Whatever happened to the dog?"

"That is almost funnier than this story. They became the best of friends. That dog loved Mac. The Clevelands end up giving the dog to him. We kept that dog until he passed just before Mac went off to basic training."

I loved Roscoe…makes me consider getting another dog. Dad and Destiny sit at the counter, neither of them speaking.

And as if she read my mind, Destiny breaks the silence. "Papa Mac, what made you share that story?"

"You have to know that both of my boys are driven. They get exactly what they want in life. Chris is money, and Mac is a protector. I think he would have continued to run from that dog had it not been for Kenneth that day. He looked past his own fear to protect his friend."

I drop to the couch. Dad's words hit the bullseye.

"Because like that story I think you're running." Dad places a hand over hers in the middle of the counter. "And know that whoever or whatever is on your heels has met its match. Mac won't let whoever it is get to you without going through him first."

I close down the security app as Dad's words roll through my mind. The truth laced in his words fit like a glove. But I never would have formulated the words in such a manner.

I'm loyal. I'm persistent. I'm responsible. And Dad's right, I'm a protector. It's what made me want to join the Marines. But I couldn't stay after losing Kenneth on that mission.

I LOOK AROUND MY SMALL PLACE. IT'S A TEMPORARY solution while I built my house. Then I'll turn this place into a guest house. But for now, it's my refuge.

I've traveled the world only to find there was no place like home. Joining the Marines right out of high school stripped me of my rebellious ways, and in its place, it left me a stronger man. But that strength came at a high cost.

My son is a protector.

Dad's words follow me throughout the day. I met with a few auctioneers and visited a few small auto dealers thanks to some classified ads. I slowly make my way back to Madison Grove, ready to confront my ole lady.

I had no intentions of starting a relationship with anyone. I was content with working alongside Dad, hanging out with Chris a few times a week and retreating to my shop. Behind closed doors, I can work for hours alone. There are no bombs to contend with, no need for predator drones to watch my back, and no Destiny disrupting the solitude I thought I wanted.

It only took her hanging out with me in my shop to realize how much I love her company. She knows how to fill the space with her chatter, requiring very little input from me. Or she sits in the chair curled up with a book, passing tools as needed. It was an easy peace I can get used to. But do I want it?

I exit the highway. I feel the silly grin on my face just from the thought of driving home to Destiny. The weight of the unknown doesn't compare to the idea of willingly sitting back and letting her believe that I don't care. I care. More than I'd like to admit. And I want her to stay.

My Camaro rumbles and obeys the pressure of my foot as I increase my speed. I glance at the dash clock. It's almost five o'clock, and if I hurry, I can talk to her before she leaves. I pull out my cell phone and dial the shop.

"Reese & Sons, this is Destiny speaking, how can I help you?"

I can think of a million ways for her to help me. But I'll start at the beginning, "Call Faith and tell her I'm taking you home."

CHAPTER SEVENTEEN

A TRICKLE OF ANTICIPATION RUNS THROUGH MY VEINS THE moment I disconnect the call. I called Faith, and now I sit in the quiet shop waiting for Mac. Hearing his voice caused my heart to hiccup and race because I've missed him. Then I hear the rumble of his car outside and the internal debate stops. I grab my backpack, unable to stop my feet.

I push the door open, and he's here. His thick dark hair pushed back from his face, his strong jaw covered in a bed of hair with a mustache and my eyes find his. Mac has a way of making me feel like I'm the only woman in the world. And the intensity in his dark eyes turns darker, igniting a yearning.

"Come here, Angel."

I free my hands and close the space between us. He cups my face, and his eyes heavily slide closed. I inhale, and Mac crawls into my pores, steeping my soul with him. The smell of his minty breath. The warm notes of his cologne. Then the brush of his exhale across my parted lips, I'm far past teasing, and I consider begging as the hum of my core makes the inevitable clear.

I want him.

"Ethan…"

He smiles with his lips hovering, almost touching, but not touching enough. "Yes, Angel."

"Can I have you?"

"Destiny…" He jerks back, his eyes searching to the depths reaching down to my soul and returning ablaze with desire. His mouth is on mine, telling me without words that this is much more than a kiss. This is him staking his claim on my heart, and he can have it. All of it.

He ravishes me, and I lean in taking every kiss, every lick, as our tongues war. How can he be so gentle yet strong? So, demanding yet leisurely?

I've known pain and heartache, and it felt nothing like this.

"Stay with me tonight."

I nod. Mac walks me to the car opening the door. I snap my belt, and he's beside me. He pulls my chin, and I kiss him, deepening before he turns his attention to the road.

"Roll the window up."

He cranks on the air conditioner, and we take a path heading deeper into the property at full speed. The gravel and rocks kick up, pinging the side of the car, stirring up a cloud of dust. I laugh as we race down a new direction. He wraps a hand around my thigh beneath my skirt, and I inhale. His hand is higher up my leg than before, spreading the length until his finger brushes my heat. By instinct I roll my hips forward, sure he feels the moisture. He continues his journey down the road, the trees fly by, and his hand slips beneath the elastic of my panties and cups my heat.

I gasp. My eyes slide closed, feeling the speed of the car and the motion of his fingers on my tingling pearl. I squeeze my legs holding his hand captive.

The car slams to a stop. We jerk, and the dust swirls around the car filled with our labored breathing.

"We have to talk."

"We will." I assure him rolling against his hand, and his eyes find mine.

"Destiny…" His husky tone makes me crawl over the partition and I lower to his lap. He pushes up the front of my dress, pulling it over my head. I'm sitting in his lap in my bra and panties. I cover myself, looking side to side, remembering we're outside.

"Don't worry, there's no one on this land but you and me and God." He slips a finger over the delicate lace, finding my nipple with his tongue. I groan, rolling his hardness against the fire, craving to feel more of his thickness.

Fuck... I'm in trouble.

He gives the more I give. I'm leaning with the steering wheel in my back. He grips my hips, thrusting while suckling. Then his thumb brushes my clit.

"Ethan..."

He chuckles, not releasing my nipple. The concentrated effort of his motions—stroking, rubbing, and sucking has me going insane. I run my hands through his hair with my eyes closed so tight I see hints of stars. I slip my hands between my thighs and play with the tip of his head as the stars shine brighter.

The tension builds. Heavy breathing. Deep strokes.

My head falls back as I scream his name and Mac groans.

CHAPTER EIGHTEEN

MAC CARRIES ME INSIDE. I HOLD MY DRESS AGAINST THE front of me until we enter his house. We pass through the living room, and he lays me on a bed. I glance around, and I'm in the center of a large bed.

"This bed is humongous."

He laughs and removes his shirt. "It's custom."

My eyes trace the valleys defining his washboard stomach. He unbuttons his pants, pushing them down to the floor. My mouth waters. He's fully aroused, thick and ready between his lean thighs. He produces a condom.

"I want nothing more than to make love to you." He walks to the edge of the bed standing between my legs. He said, *love*. Is that possible?

Yes. I've questioned my feelings for Mac while apart. I considered if he's a rebound. I wondered if it's the teenager in me living my fantasy. I even questioned if Papa Mac's story persuaded my heart to open and accept the love I feel for Mac. But after digging, I accept that I sought financial security over the character with my boyfriends in the past and I paid a high cost.

But nothing, and I mean nothing, about them and Mac belong in the same thought. He is caring and supportive. He praises me for the work I've done. He encourages me to find more clients. He hasn't wavered in his support even after I pushed him away, well, except for maybe the hard edges I see creep into his eyes from time to time.

I know there's more. But pushing him to tell his secrets would mean I'd have to spill mine and I'm not ready for that.

"Where are you, Angel?"

"I'm with you." I sit up, turning my mouth up for him to kiss me again. He does, and I close my eyes, praying to cherish this feeling for as long as I can. "Ethan..."

"Yes, baby." He crawls on the bed, taking me with him. I stare in his eyes for a while, hoping my questions won't ruin the moment. I divert my gaze to our laced fingers.

"I want you to make love to me. But not before we talk. Just in case..."

"In case what?" He turns my face to him. "I'm not changing my mind. I didn't change my mind before either. I wanted to give you the space you needed. But I never stopped wanting you. There's only one thing that can make me walk away."

"And what's that?"

"You saying you don't want me. I can't force you, Destiny. Then I'd be worse than the man that's been keeping us apart. I hate that you trust him more than you trust me, but I figure we'll get better with time."

"It's not that I trust him more—" He covers my mouth with a soft kiss. I pull back looking into his eyes.

"Don't lie to me and don't tell me to go. Everything else, I can deal with."

I nod, and I follow my heart. "I met my ex at a club in Dallas. He was the security guard hired by the owners since he did it as an off-duty police officer."

"He's a cop?" His eyebrows raise in shock.

"Yes, he was a cop then, and now he's a plainclothes homicide detective." I try not to ignore the questions in his eyes. This is hard enough, so I lay my head on his chest, and he falls back. "He kept sneaking over to the table, buying me drinks. We danced together on his break. And that was the nature of our relationship for a while. I'd see him at the club, and we'd flirt and drink and dance. Then one night I was heading home after a date, and he was waiting in the parking lot of my apartment."

He stops playing with the end of my braid. "How'd he know where you lived?"

"I didn't ask then, and I should have. Shit, it should have been a big fucking warning sign. But I found it flattering that he went through all the trouble to find me. I was so stupid."

He kisses the top of my head. "We all do things that we'd change if given the opportunity."

"Even you?" I ask.

"Even me. I regret asking Kenneth to join me in the military under the buddy program. Now, I have to wonder if he'd be alive to care for his son and wife if I hadn't."

I kiss his chest and continue. "Then he'd pop up here and there. I'd have a flat tire. He'd be there. I'd come out of school. He'd be there. Just randomly he'd appear."

"So, he was stalking you?"

"Not...not stalking." I glance up into his eyes. "Do you think he was stalking me?"

"How'd he know your address? Or that your tire was flat? That seems like more than coincidence. He was following you."

I fall silent. "I thought it was creepy at first, but he'd bring lunch or flowers or little things that made me feel special. We started going out, and things progressed fast. He said he wanted to marry me and build us a house, and he made all of these promises. Promises of things I never had, and like a fool, I fell for it. Then he started changing. I started noticing the differences when he didn't want me to hang out with my friends.

"But he said it was so I could focus on getting my college degree, which he paid for to kept me busy. Before I knew it, three years had passed. His suggestions became demands. And when I realized who he was, I tried to leave. Then..."

"Then what?" Mac's voice holds a deadly edge.

"He hit me."

"Are we talking pushing or fist punch? Both are bad but..." His body is tense beneath me.

"In the beginning, it was him roughing me up for my smart remarks or second-guessing him. Overtime it escalated. A guy would say good morning to me in the store. The moment we'd make it home he'd slap me or punch me accusing me of flirting. He'd choke me until I blacked out. He'd make sure to hit me in places hidden beneath my clothes."

"Did you ever report it?"

"I did once."

I EXHALE. 'HIS BEST FRIENDS ARE COPS TOO. ONE NIGHT after going to the club, he had a jealous tantrum about me always flirting with guys and rubbing my ass over them. We were almost home. I yelled and cursed him out. Then he punched me, not like before. My head hit the window, and I blacked out. That was just the beginning. By the time he was done, I couldn't recognize myself for weeks."

"What about a doctor?"

"He had a private physician come to the house. The moment I could speak clearly, I tried to tell his friends. He said he'd kill me if he didn't love me so much. This was during the time he built the house. So, he moved me while I was recovering under the care of the private doctor. And when I finally healed, I was a prisoner in his home."

Mac sits up. I've never told anyone the details. On the one hand, it feels good to finally tell someone, but on the other, I wonder how could I have been so foolish? Why did I think that was love?

"And the doctor never reported it?"

"No."

"And prisoner, as in…" His eyes blaze, not with passion, but rage.

"I couldn't leave the house without him. The house was outside the city. I didn't drive then, so it left me at home. So, he'd lock me inside while he worked, and his cop friends guarded the house."

"But you got away."

"I ran every chance I got, but he always found me.

This is the longest I've been away from him." I curl my knees to my chest and chew on the inside of my cheek.

"And this is why you wanted to leave Madison Grove?"

"Yes. I never told him about Faith or living here. He comes from a wealthy family that covers his tracks. The last thing I need is him hunting down Faith or worse…"

"Worse? What's worse than him beating you?"

"Death."

CHAPTER NINETEEN

I CONTAIN MY FEELING AND AIM TO SCRUB THE THOUGHTS of this guy from her mind. He's not the only one with connections, but first I have to take care of my angel.

I lower her back. "Do you believe that I won't hurt you?"

She nods. Her answer pleases me. I kiss her, but unlike before, I want to sear the images of every guy before me from her mind.

I cover her body with mine and bring us eye to eye. "Do you believe that I'm all yours?

Destiny searches my eyes, darting from left to right. "Why?" she whispers.

"Because you're caring and kind, you think about others before yourself, because I can't fathom how I lived this long without you in my life."

Her eyes water with tears. I kiss each one away. I

cover myself and position my body between her legs. Then her words come back to mind, and I plead, "Can I have you?"

"Yes."

I enter her. Her body fits me like a glove destined before time as I rock us steady. I make a commitment in my heart with each stroke. My heart, body, and soul declare my love for her over and over. And I won't stop telling her until she believes me until she tires of hearing because I'll never tire of saying it. I whisper this commitment over every scar, every peak, every valley.

She rides, whimpering, screaming, and I'm glad I don't have neighbors for miles. Our bodies are one, and I give Destiny my heart, praying I'm not asking too much.

"Ethan…" she says between gasps.

"Call me Ethan again." I fold her legs up.

"Ethan…" Her eyes roll back, and I thrust deeper. Her back arches off the mattress, and her eyes snap to mine. And I see it, her soul exploring the galaxy, and I force myself to slow down, but it feels fucking amazing. I grit my teeth, and our release shakes heaven and earth.

I collapse beside Destiny and pull her body to me. Her eyes struggle to remain open, and at the moment her eyes find mine, I whisper, "I love you."

"I love you too."

CHAPTER TWENTY

My body doesn't feel like my body. We made love all night, and now we're rushing to get to the shop. He takes me by Faith's house to grab clothes, and we head back, kissing at every stop sign, and we manage a little touchy-feely session at the traffic light.

I shower at Mac's and dress quickly. We have a long day ahead. He has several car deliveries, and I'm meeting with Kathryn about her website while Mac and Little Kenny spend an hour or so working on his surprise birthday car.

We make it back to the shop. I go to my office but not before Mac kisses me senseless and whispers, "I love you, Destiny."

"Will I ever tire of hearing it?" I ask, happy that for once I got it right.

"I hope not because I plan to tell you every chance I

get." I lean into his body and kiss him, slipping him a little tongue.

"You better watch out." He smacks my ass, and I laugh. "I might have to follow you to your office and close the blinds."

"Don't threaten me with a good time. After last night, I'll be sneaking around corners begging for a taste."

He pulls me to him, kissing the back of my neck. "I got all the samples you need. Just ask."

"I'll remember that." I laugh, turning off to my office and remember Papa Mac's coffee. I get it started and pour Mac a mug then myself. He smacks a kiss on my lips, and I head back to my office.

I'm floating on the clouds, but I need to land this baby, I have work to do. I start with bringing up the final revisions for the full Reese & Son's website. I need Mac's approval after completing the payment portal, adding the pictures of the first round of cars available for sale, and establishing the social media accounts.

I dance in my chair because he hasn't seen the pictures I have of the cars thanks to his crew. They pulled out each one and helped me capture the necessary angles to appeal to buyers. Once he approves, I can slowly add them to their accounts. I've also researched other local businesses to tag and hopefully generate a little buzz for their new website. Once that's all done, I print the most recent contact form submissions for car inquiries submitted through the website.

I gather the files neatly and walk to Mac's office. I turn on the light and head tohis inbox. His office is immaculate. He may have left the military, but Mac is still a Marine at heart. I extend a hand to drop the papers in the basket when I notice a card next to his office phone.

He found me.

The pages in my hand miss the basket and tumble to the floor as my hands cup my mouth to suppress the whimper lodged in my throat. How? How had Ryan found me?

I reach for the card from the Dallas Police Department.

"Hey what' cha got there?"

I jump, turning to see Mac. My chest rises and falls in quick spurts. What am I going to do? I'm spinning back and forth like my thoughts. I stop shoving the card towards Mac, "Is he in Madison Grove?"

"Who? Angel, what's wrong?" His hands are securely on my shoulders, but a fog falls over my eyes, and it makes it hard for me to pull out of the haze in my mind. *What will I do?*

"Destiny. Destiny!" Mac sounds miles away, and the slight shake of my body brings my eyes to his.

I step back, heading for the door. I don't need to

pack my stuff. Faith can ship it to me. Thank God I kept the truck in the storage out back. I contemplated how to get rid of it, but I'll use it to cross the state lines into New Mexico and take a bus or train to California.

Mac grabs my wrists, stopping my departure. "Where are you going? What just happened?" He glances at the card on the floor. "Do you know him?"

"Mac, I gotta go. I can't stay here." I pull my arm free and head to my office. *My office.* It won't be my office anymore. I'll start over. I pull my backpack from the bottom drawer, and I'm stopped by Mac in the doorway.

"Destiny, you have to tell me what is going on."

I can't look at him. I can't stare into his eyes and walk away again. The last time almost killed me. I feel a connection with Mac, unlike anything I've experienced in all of my life.

After losing my sisters, I became a loner. Even in relationships, I found ways to erect walls and hide safely behind them. But with him that's impossible. My walls seem intrusive and a barrier from the warmth he so freely gives.

Mac reaches for me, and I coil. He retracts his hand but remains unmoved from blocking the door like an armored truck ready for war. His dark smoky brown eyes plead with me. I squeeze my eyes shut, holding my backpack against my chest.

Mac won't step aside, but unlike the men, in my past,

I know he won't harm me. Can he help keep me safe from Ryan? And can I keep him safe from Ryan's backlash? I didn't think about that before. What if Ryan tries to harm Mac...or Papa Mac...or he finds Faith?

I freeze. My brain is overloaded, and I stare blankly into Mac's eyes. I'm tired of doing this alone.

My son is a protector. Papa Mac's words burst through my defenses.

"Destiny, you can't keep running. Stay and let me help you. There's no reason for you to leave your business, your sister, or me. I love you, Jelly Bean."

"But..." I hate crying. I glance away, embarrassed. I feel weak, and I'm frustrated as fuck because I'm tired. Why do I have to give up the people who love me and that I love?

"Angel, don't cry. Tell me what's going on, and I'll protect you with my life."

Maybe if I tell him, he'll see why I have to leave. He'll see it's best to keep everyone safe.

"This is Ryan, my ex-boyfriend." I thrust the card in his direction and collapse into the chair.

I can't stop shaking. How foolish am I to believe that I outwitted Ryan?

Looking back, the signs were everywhere. But I overlooked them until it was too late. He found me then, he found me now. I stand with the realization that Ryan won't stop until I go back. He won't let me leave. How many times had he told me, "You belong to me?"

The words grip my heart like a tight fist, and I glance at the card in Mac's hand. He doesn't deserve this. Not if I really love him and care for him. It's best to leave now. I stand up and take the steps needed to sever the invisible hold Mac has on me.

"Destiny listen to me. Please listen to me."

He asks, not demands. Another sign of the type of man he is, and I can't deny him.

I face him. The etch of worry I expect to see is nowhere to be found. I search his eyes, and the edge of anger I see is familiar. I stumble back a few steps, but I can't tear my gaze from his.

I HAVE A CHOICE. I CAN LET HER LEAVE AND MOVE ON with my quiet, basic, pre-Destiny life. Or I can trust the man I know I am. I won't let anyone harm her.

I glance at the card erecting a silent war between us. I wish I could turn back the hands of time and placed the card inside my desk. But then we wouldn't be standing here. I can't hit an invisible target, but I'm a sharpshooter, and this son-of-a-bitch is mine. This is the opportunity I need to ensure Destiny stays here with me where she belongs, and I'm taking it.

I step closer to Destiny thankful that she doesn't coil from my touch. Her defensive stance makes me want to fold her into my arms. That will be impossible with her standing on the other side of the room.

All the years of training surface and my new mission is taking down Ryan. I don't know the man, but he's disrupting my future with Destiny because I know this woman is my future and I'm not stopping until we give it a fair shot. We deserve this.

Dad's words surface when I need him the most. "Let me protect you."

There's a slight angle of her head and her eyes. I have her attention. I'll use my skills from recon, whether with weapons or my bare hands to keep her safe and to remove the fear from her eyes.

"Mac, you don't know him."

"But I know me."

I use her delayed response to slide an arm around her waist and do what I wanted since I entered my office—hold her. She's stiff, and I hold her tighter, placing a soft kiss at the base of her neck. Her shoulders relax, then her head rests on my chest. I tuck her tight beneath my chin, rubbing her back and whisper softly in her ear. "I love you, Destiny. Trust that I won't let him hurt you again. I'll protect you with my life."

Destiny buckles in my arms, and I scoop her up and carry her to the chair. I sit with her across my lap as her tears flow. Her body trembles in my arms, and this Ryan character will pay for every tear that drops from her eyes. To block out the rage building beneath the surface, I call on the Marine in me. I need to rid my woman of this man and give us a fresh start.

"Angel, tell me everything."

CHAPTER TWENTY-ONE

I FEATHER A KISS ACROSS MAC'S NECK, RUNNING MY hands through his hair. He reaches for a tissue and dries my face before kissing me softly. The same arms I admired while he works on his beautiful cars are the same wrapped around me like a barricade blocking out all that ails me. I snuggle closer, and he tightens his hold.

I won't dare look in his face. I take a deep breath. I've considered how to tell him this part of my story. But I couldn't form the words. Every version of my story made me sound spoiled and entitled. I was after the big fish, and I caught exactly what I aimed for—a rich man to take care of me and whisk me away. I hated growing up poor and wanted a life of leisure without worrying about whether I'd eat or have the money to support myself. But where had my selfish ambition led me... back home in Madison Grove.

I hate that it took this to bring me back but sitting in Mac's arms made my hardship and bad choices a little easier to bear.

"I don't know where to begin, so I'll start with Granny's death. I think you were away at college. Faith was placed with a family here. But Hope and I were shipped off. I was moved between so many homes that I lost count. So, the moment I graduated, I saved my money and bought a bus ticket. I hopped on the first thing smoking." The scratchy tone of my voice sounds different, because it's void of the bitterness that once controlled my heart. "I never quite connected with anyone, and I didn't have my sisters. So, I was like fuck it. I became a loner and embraced being an outsider." I shrug, fiddling with the neckline of his Reese & Sons shirt.

"For the life of me, I don't know what I expected. It started a cycle of partying, working, moving. Partying, working, moving." I used my hand to show the vicious cycle. At the time, it was fun, I guess. But nothing about it ever felt like the peace I'm experiencing with Mac.

"I'd drink and use whatever drugs available. Then I'd get tired of whatever man I'd latched on to, and I'd move on." The muscles in his arms quiver beneath me. But starting with the truth seems like the only way to put this behind me for good. And maybe sharing it with Mac will help me unearth why I kept chasing the wrong guys. Men who saw me as a possession—unlike Mac, who makes me feel cherished.

"I went to Houston, Atlanta, New Orleans, and even spent a few years in New York. Then a few years ago, I wanted to move back to Texas, so I went to Dallas. I had a few friends I'd managed to stay in touch with and moved there with a girlfriend."

Mac nods here and there but remains quiet.

"I went out one Friday night as usual. My friend and I had a disagreement, and I was itching to move again. So, I went to the club to dance off my blues or drown them in booze." My laugh isn't one of humor. Booze had been my drug of choice. I could drink most women *and men* under the table.

"I saw Ryan with a few of his friends, and he wasn't working."

I remember that night, the night I really saw Ryan. I didn't recognize him because he wasn't in his uniform. And he looked out of place in the club. He was in dress pants and a button-up, not jeans and tees like the rest of the crowd. His blue eyes, baby face and sandy blond hair amid fades, the hues of brown skin, and an environment known to get rowdy without notice. He was calm and laughing with his boys. It was like a spotlight pointed him out to me. It had been Mike that approached asking to buy me a drink. But it was Ryan that had my eye.

"We talked that night until the club closed. He took

my number, and we talked all the way home by phone." I thought it was kind of magical at the time. And the story still holds hints of the fairytale that lingered or resurfaced to give me hope, but it never lasted.

"We dated, and I learned he was a detective. I thought I'd finally found a good one after dealing with so many losers. After my girlfriend and I had a big blowout, he offered to let me stay in his guest room. I took the offer."

"Then the progression of our relationship happened like I told you last night. First, he didn't want to party. Then it was my friends, he didn't like my friends. Then he found us a new beautiful home outside the city. He ensured I had everything I ever wanted in the walls of our house. It was something out of a high-to-do magazine with all the bells and whistles. I even learned to drive, and he bought me a Benz. But I was a prisoner, and I didn't see it happening."

I twist at the hem of my skirt, wrapping and unwrapping it around my finger. I look back over my memories and try to pinpoint the moment it all changed. Mac remains silent, softly brushing my arm with his thumb.

"See what?" His cheek rests on top of my head.

I shrug. I dive back into the darkness of my memories to the night when my hopes were doused. And that night jumps forward. I inadvertently gasp, and Mac tightened his hold on me.

"The moment that changed us. But as I think about it, maybe it never changed because it was what it always had been." A tingle passes through me. Much like Ryan, the house we shared conjured up polar opposites. The interior design, arranged to please the eyes, was modern and appealing. A harsh reality was embedded in the grains of the dark wood furniture. It was magnificent, and I was held captive by the very thing I crave for my entire life...a house. A house to call home.

"What was it?" Mac interrupted my thoughts. I'd spent so much time pointing the finger at Ryan and his faults that I hadn't noticed my part in it. Away from the drinking and partying, I realize I had changed, and Ryan had remained the same.

"My desire to have a place of my own, a home, allowed him to entice me with his beautiful dungeon."

CHAPTER TWENTY-TWO

SHARING THE DETAILS ABOUT MY LIFE BEFORE MOVING back to Madison Grove freed me. Mac was no less caring and attentive, but it felt like he was moving away from me. After another late night working at the shop, he drops me off at Faith's place.

Our long talk about Ryan happened a couple of weeks ago. Ryan never returned Mac's phone call. But we're still not taking any chances. So, either Mac, Chris, or Faith drive me to and from work, and I'm never left alone for long.

"You're here." He walks me to the door.

Faith's car isn't in the driveway. She's back to spending all her time at the boutique since the grand opening is tomorrow. Tonight, I'm taking some time off, and I'm working all day tomorrow to assist with the finishing touches. I stare at the man that promised to protect me. He scans the street before settling his eyes on me. I step forward and wrap my arms around his waist.

Mac holds me. I rest my head on his chest, smelling the mix of sweat and the faint scent of his cologne. I close my eyes, wondering if he will turn me down again. For the last few nights I've invited him in, but he's declined.

"Stay a while," I mumble into his chest, snuggling into his chest. It's perfect right here as he tightens his hold.

"Not tonight." He tugs on one of my braids.

"Did I do something wrong?" I lean back to search his face in the porch light. His handsome face melts my insides. His eyes brush past mine with a distance I knew quite well. I've been working up the courage to ask, afraid of his response. Maybe I told him too much. Perhaps he changed his mind. I'm far from ordinary. I'm better, but not whole. However, I'm working hard to make the necessary changes to have a full life in Madison Grove, and I want it with him.

"No, nothing's wrong, I'm just tired. Between getting this custom car ready for Little Kenny and helping Faith with the grand opening, I'm exhausted." He smiles.

"Are you sure?"

He nods.

I stand back and give him my house keys. He opens

the door and steps inside to check out the place like he does every night. Once he's satisfied, he returns and kisses me on the cheek.

"Lock the door behind me." And he's gone.

"Love you," I whisper to the closed door. I want to follow him and shake it out of him. Instead, I turn to the kitchen following the growl of my stomach. We should have some leftovers from Sunday dinner in the refrigerator. The worse part of the distance with Mac is having him near only to experience the light pecks on my cheek or forehead. And we haven't made love since I told him about Ryan.

Melancholy settles over me. I said I'd trust him. That includes taking his word. Right? I sigh—*men*.

I stop and pull out my cellphone. *Thanks, love you.* I wait, and instead of letting my mind run wild, I focus on food.

I open the refrigerator and lower my head inside. I remove the containers of fried chicken, mashed potatoes, and corn on the cob. I got tired of pizza and burgers. I cooked dinner on Sunday, and it feels great to have real food.

I stack one on top of the other and use my chin to keep them from tumbling over. I sit them on the counter next to the microwave. I open the door and placed the chicken in first.

I work my magic, and after a while, I have my

dinner. I found a cold soda in the back of the refrigerator, and now I'm ready to Netflix and Chill with my damn self. I laugh and put my plate on the coffee table, when I hear a knock. I shift my eyes toward the living room. I lick the chicken flavor from my fingers and wipe my hands off with a napkin.

Mac. I walk over to the door with an expectant smile. He came back. I pull open the door, and it's him.

I LEAVE TOWN HEADING HOME, AND SOMETHING TELLS ME to turn back. It's been torture trying to keep Destiny at a distance. With every brush of her hand, or the way she leans into me it makes my desire to have her increase.

We worked out a schedule of getting her around and keeping her safe, but the shadows of her words cause me to doubt. What if she's latching on to me only to leave? That seems to be her M.O.

My phone chimes and I pull to the side of the road. It's from Destiny, *Thanks, love you.*

I pull over on the shoulder of the old country road and call my brother. He's been traveling in and out of town to secure investors for another project. I haven't had a chance to catch up with him.

"What's up, Mac?" he calls out.

"I'm sitting in the dark on the side of the road, questioning life. I think I'm trippin'."

"And that's new?"

"I'm serious, Chris. This shit with Destiny has me wondering if... I don't know what the hell I'm thinking." I drop my head back.

"Do you love her?"

"Yes, but—"

"I'm sorry, you can't add the but. Aren't you the one that told me to man-the-fuck up and pursue Faith or leave her alone?"

"I don't like it when you use my words against me."

"Tough. I live for the days I can turn your words around. It's like having ice cream for breakfast. The Cowboys winning the Super Bowl. Rihanna wearing that little braless number with her breast—"

"Okay...I think I get the point." I scrub my hand over my face a few times.

"I think your loyalty stops you from living a full life. You're balancing the folks, Kenneth's memory, helping Kathryn, Little Kenny. At some point, your happiness must factor into the equation, or you'll become a casualty of your good intentions. Because regardless of how fucked up Destiny's situation is, you love that woman and good women don't stay single long."

This is a hard pill to swallow. I can't see my Angel

with another guy, kissing another guy, making love to…
I hook a U-turn. I'm going back.

"And Faith?" I ask.

"Mac, I'm playing a high stakes game hoping that when I'm done conquering the world Faith will still let me kiss her when I want to." His voice fades off.

"Is it worth it?"

"The verdict is still out on that one."

"So, besides being a *perv* for staring at Rihanna's tits. Any advice?"

"Hey, I didn't call them tits but grown-ass woman breasts. Did you see that shirt?" I can see his smile from here.

"Talk, Chris, and not about Rihanna's breast."

Chris gives a hearty laugh. "Damn, you're a tough crowd. My advice is don't be so busy protecting everyone else that you miss out on your chance at happiness."

"Damn. That's actually good advice." I stare at my cellphone. Did Chris just go deep on me?

"I had that shit stored for a rainy day."

The silence hangs for a second, and we laugh. Chris is my best friend and my brother in one. To know he's helping me and not trusting his heart to pursue Faith has me curious.

"Thanks for pulling it out. But I have a question, why

are you fighting your feelings for Faith? She's an amazing woman."

"Yeah, I could ask you the same. But I'm done being Yoda for the day. I guess…" He exhales. "What if I don't make her happy? Destiny is dealing with some crazy ex. But at least she went out, searched the world, and realized this is home. But Faith has only known Madison Grove and what if…I don't know… What if it turns out that I'm just the available cat across the street?"

I didn't expect that response. "Trust your love for her."

"I will if you will."

CHAPTER TWENTY-THREE

I PARK AT THE END OF THE BLOCK AND RECHECK THE address. That's the house. I sit and light a cigar. I wait watching the traffic. This is a quiet street. Her sister usually returns close to midnight, according to the surveillance. Let's see if I can get a little quality time with Dez. I reach to turn the key over, and the Camaro returns.

CHAPTER TWENTY-FOUR

"Can I come in?" I stand back, and Mac walks inside.

"Would you like something to eat?"

"Do you mind sharing yours?" His smile is slow, and I'm surprised.

"Are you flirting with me?" I place a hand on my hip. I haven't seen this man for a minute. And he seems nervous. "You came to break it off."

"No." But he can't look me in the eyes. "I came to apologize. Sit with me."

I walk over, and we sit on the couch. Mac leans forward.

"What is it? You're scaring me."

"I asked you to be honest with me, and your truth made me uncertain of where I stand with you."

I glance at him sideways. "What do you mean? I told you everything."

"Yeah, but how do I know you're not biding your time until you leave? And then what? You run off, and I don't see you for another fifteen years."

"That's fucked up, Mac."

"Destiny, I'm a man. A man who loves the hell out of you. And knowing that I can drive up to the shop or over here to see my ole lady and she's gone. That's fucked up."

"Then why ask me to be honest if you're just going to use it against me?" I slide away from him. I can't believe him. Then Mac slips his hand beneath my legs and places me on his lap. I cross my arms but don't move. This is as close as he's been in almost two weeks. I missed him. And I love this man like my next breath, which scares the shit out of me. Because love hasn't been kind to me, but Mac has...until now.

"Angel, I'm sorry." he whispers kissing my neck, and he wraps his arms around me.

"Did Papa Mac tell you to apologize?"

"No."

"Faith?"

"No. My heart... and Chris."

"Chris! It took Chris to get you back here." I move to stand up, and Mac makes a stealth move. We're standing, and my legs are wrapped around his waist. "What did Chris say?"

"You don't want to know." He glances away, and I cup

his face in my hands, bringing his beautiful eyes back to mine.

"Tell me." I see the love there even if he's fighting it. Is this what real love feels like? When you can't eat, can't sleep, don't want him near, but I don't want him far away either.

"Before or after Rihanna's tits?"

"Ethan McKenzie, put me down. Talking about another woman's breasts to apologize to me."

"Angel, you asked. I promise you Chris' advice had Rihanna's—"

"Say it again, and you and Chris are going to be on my shit list."

He snaps his mouth closed. The heat in his eyes emerges, and I can't look at him. "You're sexy when you're mad."

"Mac..."

"It's that little vein throbbing. The pucker of your mouth." He leans forward and sweeps his tongue between my lips, and I capture it. The kiss is quick and electric. He doesn't stop until I'm breathless, and my back is against the wall. "I missed you."

I roll my eyes. And look over his shoulder. "Did I scare you off?" I whisper.

"No, I was scared of losing you." He stares at me, waiting for my next response. "I love you, and I've never loved a woman as much as I love you. So, knowing that you hopped on a bus and never returned shook me a little."

"A little?"

He shrugs. "A lot."

"And what was Chris' advice?" I give him a stern look.

"He said to trust my love for you."

"Do you?" This man loves me. I feel it, and he's letting me in. I see for the first time that we're both stretching to have something we've never had before.

Real love.

"I do. I want to build a life with you. Give you the home you want. Have some babies. Grow old with you. A dog."

"I want that too."

His mouth covers mine. Clothes fly left and right before we end up in my room with him deep inside me. Our declarations of love ring truer that before. He makes love to me, and before he falls asleep, I ask. "What happened to Kenneth?"

Mac kisses my cheek and pulls me to him. I snuggle closer, waiting for the missing piece of this puzzle.

"He died. I led a group into a secret mission. Seven men went in. Six went out." He falls deathly silent. "I ensured the safety of all my men except my best friend."

I can't understand his pain, but I can love him. I

guess loss is part of our lives and we have to find a way to go on.

"Ethan you're an amazing uncle, and you look after Kathryn like she's your sister. And you care for my sister like she's your family. You served your country, now you serve this town. You even opened your business and heart to take in a runaway. I think it's safe to say, you can stop punishing yourself."

He looks over at me, and I kiss him from the bottom of my soul. They don't make men like this anymore. I'd endure the hell of my life again to have this with him.

"Angel, can we try something?" He slips me a little tongue then pulls away.

"What's that? And it better not involve Rihanna."

Mac laughs until he cries, and this is how to end a night.

"No, really." I dry his eyes the way he's done mine. "Move in with me."

"I..."

"It's small but..."

"Ethan, I don't care about the size. I just want you. That's it."

"Well, you got me. I'm all yours, and I love you more than muscle cars." His eyes are filled with humor but beneath is a glint of forever.

"Yes, Ethan, I'll move in."

We seal the deal with a kiss, and I fall back. He's near sleep and curiosity is killing me.

"Mac?"

"Hum."

"What did Chris say about Rihanna's tits?"

The roar of his laughter fills the house and my heart. I'm so glad I came back to Madison Grove.

MAC KISSES ME BEFORE DAWN AND HEADS OUT. I ROLL over, mentally preparing for a full day at the boutique. I walk to Faith's room, and it's empty. I call her, and she says Chris is on his way to pick me up.

I rush to get dressed. What's Chris doing at the boutique this early in the morning? Nosiness makes me work faster. I shower and dress in my official Faith's Boutique shirt and a new skirt when I hear the doorbell.

"Coming." I throw on my backpack and open the door. "Just a second let me grab the cake." I turn, and the realization hits me. *What's he doing here?*

A gun appears. "You won't need it. It's time to go."

CHAPTER TWENTY-FIVE

I RUN TO MY PLACE AND NOTICE AN UNFAMILIAR CAR OFF the road. I don't give it much thought and keep going. I promised Destiny and Faith I'd help at the boutique. But I need to change clothes and pick up Little Kenny and Kathryn.

I run around, and we make it to the boutique. I circle the block, trying to find a place to park. The party doesn't start until five, but the place is packed. I let them out in front. Minutes later, I enter and find Faith. She's beaming from ear to ear.

"Where's Destiny?" she asks.

"I thought you picked her up?" I freeze, and the sound in the room drops out. I search the crowd for Chris.

"Chris went to pick her up this morning, and she

wasn't there. We thought she was with you." Her voice shakes.

"Did you call her?" I pull out my phone dialing her number by memory. The phone rings and rings. I call again, it rings, and the line connects before it goes dead. "Call Sheriff Davis."

"Where are you going?" she yells.

"Home."

I run to my car and pray like I've never prayed before. Angel, please have your backpack. Please have your backpack.

CHAPTER TWENTY-SIX

"WHAT ARE YOU DOING HERE?" I'M BLINDFOLDED. MY hands are tied behind my back, and the last person I saw was Mike.

"I'm coming to take you home."

"Home? Where's Ryan?"

"Dead."

I gasp. "What do you mean he's dead?"

"He had a drug overdose about a week ago. I used the last of your little stash in the kitchen to finish him off."

Now my heart is racing. He killed Ryan, which means I'm free. But I'm not. "And why are you here?"

"Because I figure now that we got him out of the way, you'd finally give me a chance. He didn't deserve you. Besides, I saw you first."

"I'm sorry to hear about Ryan...wait, can you please remove the blindfold? Please." I take a deep breath. I'm playing through this scenario, hoping someone saw us leave Faith's house. And thankfully he removes it. Why am I at the junkyard? I see Ryan's truck across the way.

"Wait a minute?" Brittany appears in the side doorway. "You asked me to help because you're trying to get with her? Why you muthafucka—"

Crack!

One second she is charging in Mike's direction and the next Brittany's falling backward. My eyes dart from her to Mike, and the stench of gun smoke fills my nose. He's glaring over the gun with a sinister grimace on his face. I'm trying to figure out what the hell is going on then I see the blood spreading across Brittany's chest, and I lose it. I scream until my throat feels raw.

"Is she dead? Is she...? Why did you...? I can't believe you just killed her!" I'm bouncing around, twisting my hands, but the rope is too tight. "Somebody help me! Mac, Carl, Liz..." I call Mac and some of the crew members, but I know they can't hear me.

"Shut up, bitch, or I'll kill you too."

I snap my mouth closed. This storage building is at the back of the property. I yank on the rope, trying to free my hands because I can't let this man kill me too.

"Why are you..." He points the gun in my direction, and I get the hint.

"How does it feel?" Mike faces me as if he expects an answer. Then he starts a slow pace back and forth. "I step to you, offer to buy you a drink. And what do you do?"

He pauses, and I stare off when I see a glint of something in the shadow. I look toward the open door, wondering if I can yell loud enough for someone to hear me. But Mike continues.

"You played me. You pick him over me. Why? Because he was wearing a fucking suit in the club." He stops again. I stare blankly, ready for this monologue to be over.

"So what he's rich. I bet you wish you'd picked me now after he used your ass for a damn punching bag. Now look at him and you." His head drops back, and his laugher swirls around us.

God, please don't let me die like this.

There were days I wanted nothing more than to end my life, to end my misery. I prayed for death. But now I have something to live for, and my mistakes won't let me go.

I stare down at my lap and focus on listening for the sounds around me. I tune out the talking head because I know I saw something in the shadows near the door. I hear soft footsteps. I cock my head to the darkness, trying to see the source. Then Mike steps in front of me.

"Now, how does it feel? Ryan's dead. Brittany's dead. It's all because you're a gold digger, looking to score the fattest wallet. I bet you wish you would've chosen me now." He places a finger under my chin, turning my face to him.

Click.

"Don't touch her." He came for me.

"Mac…" I gasp as relief floods my body. I search the darkness, thankful I'm not alone.

"Angel…are you okay?"

I nod, fighting the tears threatening to fall. It's impossible to steady my erratic pulse.

Mike lifts his hand with the gun, the same one he used to kill Brittany, and before it settles near my head, a bullet cuts through the air, and he stumbles backward.

"That wasn't a request. Cut her loose." Mac's lethal tone sends chills down my spine as he steps forward. My man's warm eyes are cold and locked on Mike. Chris passes through the shadows heading in my direction with his gun trained on Mike too.

Then my hands are free. I rub my aching wrists and grab my backpack at my feet. I only have eyes for Mac. I run to him, and the yank of my hair sends me falling backward, slamming into Mike's chest.

"You should have killed me," Mike yells jamming the steel to my temple. "And you can't kill me without killing your bitch." He laughs, and I see the rage in Mac's eyes.

Mac and Chris have their guns aimed at him, but he's behind me, and I can't run.

"Get the keys." He demands, walking us to Ryan's truck.

"Mike I—"

"Get the fucking keys, or I'm killing everybody in here."

"Fine! They're in my bag." I slip my hand inside, digging around near the bottom. But the keys are inside the truck. I need to figure something out.

"I'm not letting you leave here with her," Mac says as they inch closer. But they can't shoot him without shooting me unless they aim for his head.

"Who's going to stop me?" His hot air is against my ear.

I'm pushing the contents around trying to find a weapon, and I prick my finger. *There she is.* I slip my fingers inside My Kitty and beg Mac to look at me. *Look at me, baby. Please. Guns scare the crap out of me, but this little weapon seems perfect to distract Mike and get me to Mac.*

Mac surveys the area, and his eyes slide to mine.

I mouth. *One...two...*

I punch my balled fist, armed with a knuckle weapon, stabbing into Mike's thigh. He howls in pain, releasing me. I drop to the ground and roll out of his reach. Mac takes Mike down with one shot.

The body falls within inches of me, and I scramble away, and I don't stop until I'm in Mac's arms.

"Are you okay? Angel, are you okay?"

"I am, thanks to you. I'm done running, Mac." I cradle his face in my hands. "I love you."

He holds me so tight I can't breathe, and I don't want to. We're surrounded by death, and I'm free. His mouth covers mine for a soul-stirring kiss. He's communicating without words, and I hope he knows, this is it. He's it.

"All right, kids. Break it up." Chris calls out. "I'm stepping outside to call Sheriff Davis."

Mac pulls back. "Thanks, man. Let's get you home."

"After I see Faith."

CHAPTER TWENTY-SEVEN

THE TOWN FILLS FAITH'S BOUTIQUE FOR THE GRAND opening. Destiny and I stand off to the side. Sheriff Davis took our statements, and I agreed to supply all the footage of the incident and Destiny's journal entries. My internal concerns about how I would protect her manifested in a basic solution, much like the way Destiny has revived Reese & Sons, and that's through technology. I installed security cameras inside and outside all of our structures and a tracker inside her backpack.

Loving Destiny and the imminent threat of her ex meant coming to terms with a few things. First, my post-traumatic stress disorder. Before Destiny returned, I was content with drowning out my memories of that final mission and my best friend's death in booze. But ever since the night she texted me, I didn't want to be numbed by the alcohol. I wanted to experience this new life with her and my loved ones.

Second, I had to address my concerns about keeping her safe head-on. Kenneth died on my watch. That's a fact I can't erase from my mind, but I must find a way to move on. Because fear of the past was blocking my future with Destiny. Yeah, her returning home with a crazy ex wasn't ideal, but it wasn't her fault. I guess I'd go a little insane if I lost her too. Who wouldn't? Even if this guy took it too far.

Lastly, I now realize a slight error, and that was my failure to include sensors on the larger storage units. I had the cameras mounted on all the buildings. But I only placed the security sensors on the front office and the garages. First thing Monday I'll have it extended to include all of our buildings and maybe some sensors around the perimeters of our land. Having those sensors would have alerted me sooner to Destiny's presence.

"What are you thinking about?"

I blink several times and hold her tighter to my body. I love the serene smile that crosses her face. *God, I love her.* "I'm thinking about you, Kenneth, our future."

"Heavy stuff." She cups my face.

"A little." I glance down at my little fighter. I tried to take her home, but she wouldn't have it. I grab one of her braids and run it through my hand. "Walk with me."

I lace our hands and tell Chris we're heading out for

a walk. He hugs me, and I'm thankful for my brother. He didn't hesitate to ride with me today.

"Love you, man. I'll stay until you get back," Chris says, standing off in the back far away from Faith. His eyes never stray far from her. I hope he'll come to his senses before she moves on.

My senses are still on alert so I can imagine that he feels the same. We shifted from excitement to horror upon finding Destiny. And the night ending with two dead bodies removed from our property.

"Love you too. We won't be long. Just need some fresh air, and maybe I can convince my ole lady to go home." We bump fists.

"Good luck." Destiny's eyes round and she digs an elbow in my side as we all laugh.

I open the shop door and guide Destiny out. The upgrades around town make downtown a fantastic backdrop for a romantic walk. All the shops are closed. There's no one out, and the town is officially at peace.

I stop and look at Destiny. "I have so much to tell you."

"Can I start?"

"Sure." I guide us to a bench beneath a streetlight.

"Thank you." Her tear-filled eyes hold mine. "I brought drama and danger to your doorstep. That wasn't my intent. And I understand how my sketchy past brought me to this moment. But it also brought me to you." She plays with her hands in her lap. "I'll understand if you want to hold off on moving together, but I want you to know. Madison Grove is my home because this is where you are."

Her eyes find mine.

"I love you, Ethan. Not just because you protected me, but you're showing me love and how to love and I want it all. The house, the babies, a dog...you."

Our eyes hold. She might as well stick her precious hand through the tungsten wall mounted around my heart.

"I love you too."

"I know." She runs her hands through my hair. The confidence she has in me makes me want to give her the world. And I will.

"Destiny Mitchell..." I slide off the bench until my knee touches the concrete at her feet. Her back goes stiff, and the love in her eyes is replaced with absolute shock. "Will you marry me?"

"Yes."

"I don't have the ring yet. So, hold on to these." I remove the ball chain from my neck and slip it on hers. The two sets of dog tags rest on her chest.

I wish I could describe the moment. Her hazel eyes glistening with tears of happiness. The moonlight shining on us. The gravity of tonight.

"Yeehaw!" The duet makes me chuckle. I turn around and see Chris and Dad with Mom tucked at his side.

"*Yeehaw!*" I call back.

I stand and bring my lady with me. The crowd standing outside Faith's Boutique burst into applause as we walk over. Most of the town is here, and we are surrounded by love. Faith is beaming until she stalls, staring at Chris.

"Thank you for saving my sister." It's the first time I realize Faith chews on the inside of her mouth like my lady.

Chris steps forward cupping the side of her face and brushing a tear from her eye. "I'd do anything for you."

Destiny moves toward them, and I stop her. She rolls her eyes at me. "Don't. Let them work this out."

She turns in my arms and lifts the tags to examine them. Then her head rests on my chest. I fought for this love... through the wars, through losing my best friend...through returning home and trying to piece my life together. I fought to save Destiny tonight, and her love saved me.

"Love you, Angel."

"I love you too, Mac."

We kiss, and it's the type of kiss that heals past hurts and erases past pains. The kiss signals a new beginning for us both as we build our life together in Madison Grove.

Thank you for reading *Can I Have You?!*

MAC AND DESTINY FOUND THEIR HAPPILY-EVER AFTER. Leave your review now. **HERE**.

Let me know if you'd like to see MORE from Madison Grove by leaving a message. HERE.

Read on for a sneak peek at AS YOU WISH, available now.

LEAVE A REVIEW

Did you enjoy *Can I Have You*?

Please leave a book review **HERE**. Reviews are extremely important and it helps me continue sharing my books with fellow readers.

JOIN MY NEWSLETTER

Be the FIRST to know!

Consider joining my newsletter? http://www.
janesedixon.com/subscribe Be the first to know about
releases and specials. You can unsubscribe anytime.

Is their simmering attraction enough to defeat their crusades?

Damian "The Shark" Hughes real estate billionaire lands in Houston, Texas to handle a "problem tenant" stalling his partnership with Rock Star Entertainment. But on first sight he doesn't know which he wants more, to evict her or bed her.

Imani Scott is at the end of herself and her resources for keeping the doors of Harmony Dance open. What she doesn't have time for is the sweet talking, money slinging gorgeousness from Atlanta. Her sole focus is on her students. They are depending on her and she's not to go down without a fight.

The blurred line between friend or foe...

Imani organizes a Kwanzaa benefit recital to save her studio not knowing she's sleeping with the enemy. And Damian is willing to do whatever it takes to close the deal *and* keep this ebony beauty by his side.

At odds yet drawn to each other by their undeniable chemistry, the ticking clock and a multi-million dollar development deal erect the perfect battleground.

Will they win the battle but lose the war? Or will they let love win?

**Get Your Copy on Amazon
or Read in Kindle Unlimited!**

CHAPTER ONE

"Houston we have a problem and it must be resolved by the end of the year." Soft chuckles came from around the table.

Damian Hughes was invited to a private meeting by Cameron Carter at The Ritz-Carlton with undisclosed. These types of *secret* gatherings were not new to him but Cameron had piqued his interest.

Tilting his head back Damian reached into the corners of his mind to recall the exact verbiage Cameron used—*an offer most kill for but only five receive.* His father didn't raise a fool, and he knew if Cameron said it, it was worth returning to the United States.

Damian had cleared his calendar and boarded a private plane from Dubai heading to Atlanta, Georgia. A nomad by choice, he sold his home in the States seven years ago and now hopped from state to state, continent to continent, and a part of him welcomed this meeting due to exhaustion. Working abroad had its perks but lately he missed the comforts of his home country.

His missed southern hospitality, football games, his friends and his family. Pursing the next big deal made him a wealthy man and garnered him a seat at today's meeting, apparently he wasn't doing too bad.

"What happens in this room, stays in this room." Cameron scanned the room stopping at each attendee personally. Damian nodded his agreement.

"Very well. I've invited each of you here because Bruce and I have decided to launch Rockstar Entertainment January 1st with the debut of Marques' album." Cameron stood with his hands flat on the table. "We invited each of you because you possess a skill set that we need. You *are* the absolute best of the best and in exchange for your gifts and talents we are prepared to offer you equal partnership in RSE."

"Besides friendship, what made you select the men in this room?" Damian glanced at the men huddled around the table. He sat amongst friends, which was a welcomed treat. But he felt out of place.

"It's simple. You all are at the top of your game. I want to bring business and fire back to the music industry. Back to when our fathers were rock stars and real artistry was king." Cameron stopped and faced Damian. "RSE artists will have career longevity of David

Bowie, the pop appeal of Michael Jackson, the swag of James Brown, and the soul of Marvin Gaye."

Damian always loved music, however, his specialty was real estate and development. He'd been groomed under his father and now he traveled as a freelance consultant flipping and developing residential and commercial property.

"Gentlemen, we have six months to launch the label that will put this industry on its ass." Cameron declared.

For the next four hours Damian listened as they laid out their very ambitious business plan to introduce RSE as an independent record label and artist management firm. The idea of equal partnership intrigued him. Less traveling and more time with his family in Atlanta topped his list. A family he felt disconnected from, they talked by phone frequently but his father's declining health made Damian question his professional choices.

"To the man of the hour." All eyes were now on him.

Cameron dropped a thick folder on the table and pushed it in his direction. It slid across the polished mahogany wood table; Damian stopped the file folder before it reached the glass of iced water sitting on the decorative coaster in front of him.

"I'll give you a few minutes to review it."

Damian sat forward and extended his arms to settle into reading through the documents, maybe this would make sense of it all. He glanced around once again, he only worked with the best. Yet it was rare for him to sit amongst a table of old money. They all were second and third generation wealth. Something told him this was going to be a big one.

Focusing on the task at hand he opened the folder and his breath caught at the sight of a brown skinned beauty. Her eyes leapt off the photograph and the voices of the men around the table faded into a muffled mumble.

He picked up the picture and rested his forearm against the table, examining the rich hue of her honey kissed eyes. They twinkled as if the photographer had told a joke. His eyes swept lower wondering if remnants of her laughter would show in her smile.

No, the smirk awaiting his inspection was raw sexiness, inviting him closer. He glanced back up at her eyes and decided she was seducing the camera. From her soft pout, to the long regal neck, to the soft waves flipped to the side resting on her shoulder.

"Damian." The edge of Cameron's call cut through the haze of the electric picture sending his senses into overdrive.

"Yes." Damian dropped the picture like a hot potato.

"I think I need to start again." The men around the table chuckled, the joke was on him. He turned his attention to Cameron, wishing he could erase the sexy pout from his mind. "We need to establish two compounds for a dual headquarters. One based here in Atlanta and the other in Houston."

Now Damian caught Cameron's vision. "That's why you need me."

"Yes, sir. We haven't found an appropriate location here, and we thought we had a perfect spot in Houston but it seems we've hit a glitch and I can't babysit this."

Damian could see all types of potential for this arrangement. He would have equal ownership in RSE and access to the artists for future contracts. Not to mention the commercial development he'd add to his portfolio.

"The file contains the details about the property and Imani Wright. She is owner and operator of Harmony Dance, a hold over tenant in the Houston property."

Cameron ran through the facts like an ordinary, boring grocery list. Nothing about the heat in Imani's eyes said ordinary or boring. Damian dropped his gaze again to the folder and found her bewitchery gaze waiting for him. He pushed the picture away with the tip of his index finger.

"We attempted to use a standard real estate agent for this portion of our plan. He negotiated on our behalf and then after that it seemed to go over our heads."

"Do you own the property or are you still in negotiations?"

"We own it."

Damian nodded. "Then what's the problem?"

"It seems Miss Wright is the last tenant from the previous owner and she hasn't paid rent in, last count, six months." He let out a long frustrated breath. "We were told that all tenants were provided notices to vacate and were given a 90 day notice."

"All except one." Damian stated.

"Exactly. We're at a loss as to how we should proceed. It is an inner city, non-profit serving minority students. You get my drift. We can't just swoop in and boot her out."

"Not and keep your reputation in tact."

"You got it."

"We have plans for the property that doesn't involved managing tenants. And so, here you are."

Damian nodded and flipped through the pages skimming the dates, figures, and he realized the plight before them. He leaned back computing the issues and several exit strategies for RSE.

"The way I see it, you need to sell the property to me. The last thing you need is a woman running to the press with her cute kids pointing the finger at Rockstar Entertainment and derailing the launch." He looked down again noting the address. "Let me fly out and see how we can best resolve this."

Damian made billions cleaning up real estate messes

—residential or commercial, small town or big city, domestic or abroad.

"Done. None of our names or RSE can be attached to this situation. We have too much riding on our first impression. We'll also expect you to handle the Atlanta property and any future real estate matters. But there's a catch." Cameron lowered to his chair.

"There always is." Damian crossed his hands over the folder and faced Cameron and Bruce.

"We need this finalized by the close of the year."

IMANI WRIGHT APPROACHED HARMONY DANCE. SHE parked her gifted Toyota in the spot marked "Director". The aged signed leaned to the side, but it was hers. The cool air pumping icicles in her car was the only reliable function of her twenty year old car, which was much more than she could say about her studio. She turned the fan up to maximum.

Relief coursed through her body at seeing the door free and clear of any notifications. She'd occupied her studio rent-free for almost six months. Every day driving up was like a man walking towards death row.

"No news is good news," Imani whispered and took a long drink of her 44 oz sweet tea.

"You really need to get your life in order," Adrianna Martinez said, grabbing Imani's cup, taking a long drink too. They sat in the car together staring at the front door.

"Negative Nancy please leave your comments to yourself. I'll take every day they give me." She was her best friend, partner-in-crime, and fickle unpaid employee. As usual, she was tap-dancing on Imani's last nerve.

"All you have to do is start charging them. What other studio allows students to attend classes tuition free?" Adrianna picked up the cup again and Imani snatched her tea back. She refused to share the last of her cold drink *and* listen to her pessimistic comments.

"I'm not other studios and I won't kick my students out because their parents can't afford tuition. As long as I have lights and a building, they'll have a place to dance."

Adrianna shook her head. They had this talk at least once a week. But Imani wasn't budging. Dance always made everything better in her life. She planned to give the gift of dance to whomever for as long as the good Lord allowed.

"How long are we going to sit in this car?"

Imani would show her. She turned off the ignition and reached in the back seat for her bag. She'd needed at least two clean shirts to absorb the sweat from dancing all night. She stepped out and tossed her bag across her body. Adrianna followed stopping to straighten the sign with no luck.

Fall in Houston, Texas was a scorcher. Four seasons did not exist in Texas, it was more like spring, summer, summer squared, and hurricane season. And late September was summer squared season with a slight chance of hurricanes. Today was just plain ole hot. She wiped the sweat from her forehead as they approached the door.

Imani inserted the key into the glass door and turned until she heard the click of the lock. She pulled and the metal rubbing against metal grunted but didn't budge. The door, the raggedy building, and the god-awful property was like a hell-hole on steroids. But it was all she could afford.

She planted her feet and the door groaned in compliance. The sweltering heat from inside rushed out.

"I quit!" Adrianna squealed as steam turned her straightened hair back to curly.

Imani folded over laughing. "You can't quit. Grab the trash can over there." She propped open the door. "Don't turn on the lights. Let me get the fans."

Imani went about cooling the place off. She dropped her bag and set up four large fans in the studio. She connected her iPad to the stereo and turned on some music.

Adrianna sat in front of a fan like a diva.

"So dramatic."

Imani went outside to her trunk and grabbed two
bags of ice and walked in to see Adrianna rolling out the
five-gallon beverage coolers. She unscrewed the tops
and went out back to get the water hose.

Imani poured the ice inside the containers and added
water with the hose. Then they each grabbed a side and
placed them on a six-foot table in the corner.

She knew her diva would kick into gear. The woman
had a mouth and she quit at least once a week. Imani
appreciated her.

Her studio was hot, raggedy, and much too small but
it embodied her dream. *For now.* She shook off the
thought; they would stay until the laws kicked them out.
Besides, who in their right mind would pay for this
property? She shook her head. They should pay her for
staying.

"Miss Imani come quick." She turned towards the
sound of Tiffany's voice as the students arrived for class.
The panic in her voice made the hair on Imani's neck
stand. She ran through the door just as Taj took a punch
to the jaw. Her heart dropped as his slim body tumbled
to the hot pavement.

"Get your asses out of here or I'll call the police." The
gang of teenagers laughed and ran in the opposite
direction. "And don't come back."

Imani fell to the ground scraping her knees. "Taj baby what happened?"

"I'm okay." He pushed up and out of her embrace.

Imani wanted to scream. Why did a fourteen year old boy have to grow up so fast? To live like a grown man? And how long would she be able to convince him to return to the studio instead of the streets?

"What happened?" Tears stung her eyes.

"Nothing. I'll be back for Tiff."

Tiffany and Taj Harris were siblings and as he turned to run after the boys that used his body like a punching bag, Imani had to think quick.

"If you leave, take Tiffany with you." Her voice trembled from the helplessness storming inside her. She hated using Tiffany as a pawn but it was a gamble she had to take. Him running after those boys would only lead to trouble.

Taj's rage filled eyes challenged her. "She can't go where I'm going."

"Then you need to stay here." Tiffany ducked behind Imani clutching a handful of her t-shirt, she didn't want to lose a single one of her kids; not on her watch.

Children in the inner city lived fighting battle after battle. If it wasn't fighting bullies it was looking over their shoulders for cops. The four walls of Harmony Dance provided relief, if only for a moment from their battles filling their lives with unconditional love, a safe space, and dance.

"Don't nobody wanna go in that hot-ass studio." He grimaced.

"That's cause Harmony is fiyah!"

Tiffany laughed. "Miss Imani that was corny."

Imani laughed with her, if it meant Taj was safe then corny she'd be. "Come on, I have some cold ice water in my hot-ass studio, want a cup?"

"So lame." Taj laughed.

Imani wrapped her arms around their shoulders guiding them back to the studio. The other dancers were trickling in. "Put your cups in the trash. It's time to circle up."

Harmony Dance was her life. She had to find a way to save their building. But first, it was time to dance.

CHAPTER TWO

DAMIAN ENTERED KENN'S BAR AND GRILL, A DIMLY LIT sports bar and eatery outside of Downtown Houston. The early November weather was slightly warmer and didn't require an overcoat unlike Atlanta at this time of year. He stepped to the side of the doorway, shaking off the bite of the cool breeze in the heated interior.

"Good afternoon."

"Same to you." Damian smiled at the waiter, blinking a few times as his eyes adjusted to the drastic change in lighting.

He stretched his neck to look around the room, scanning for the perfect seat. Not too close to the big screen TVs. He spotted an empty booth in the far corner and he made his way across the room, scooting past tables and occupied chairs in the aisle. The booth would provide plenty of space to spread out and work for a while. He looked over his shoulder at the bar, he was close enough to see and hear but not be seen. Glancing at his watch, he had about thirty minutes to get comfortable before the bar opened.

He placed his briefcase on the table and unloaded his files leaving an area free to eat. The place was quiet but it picked up closer to noon. The food was decent and they offered free WiFi. He had a stack of contracts to review and his iPad for research. Since arriving in Houston he'd checked into the hotel and connected with a few colleagues. He needed people on the ground with active state licenses in law and real estate to expedite his plans in a moments notice.

Satisfied with his temporary office setup he removed his jacket and draped it over his briefcase in the seat across from him. He unfastened his sleeve buttons and rolled back the stiff cuffs. He rarely exposed his tattoos but the dark room made it hard to see plus what was the likelihood that he'd see one of his business contacts in this neighborhood.

Damian sat and reviewed the menu. Following his meeting with Cameron and his new business partners, they laid out the full rollout, each man taking responsibility for his tasks.

By the end of September, an attorney drafted a limited partnership agreement through the end of the year. All parties approved the terms and conditions of their association. Then they synchronized their tasks and calendars to meet for a group signing of the official partnership agreement for Rockstar Entertainment on January 1 in Houston.

Damian's first order of business was locating a temporary office in Atlanta. The RSE partner handling music production and artist development, Bruce Daniels, had a private studio but Damian wanted them to make a strong first impression. Even in a temporary space.

He hit the ground reestablishing old contacts and nurturing new ones and secured an amazing location in midtown. It was smaller than they needed but it would serve as their makeshift headquarters, with a studio and office space in a freestanding building structure.

By mid-October Damian closed on the midtown location and leased it back to the partnership with the option to buy. He flew in an interior designer from New York to transform the vacant space into the official Rockstar Entertainment compound. It had to be grand yet simple, edgy and classic. She exceeded expectations with the modern yet classic decor in monotones with splashes of color. Damian also commissioned the artwork for an up-and-coming artist of the rockstar legends RSE esteemed.

Signing the temporary contracts felt like the first real tether back to the United States and one step closer to establishing a sense of normalcy for him. The partnerships would ensure his frequent presence in Atlanta and hopefully set the foundation to reconnect with his parents and siblings. They lived there and he called it home but in so many ways the words never quite felt appropriate, more rote than real.

He left Atlanta with plans to wash, rinse, and repeat in Houston. He had given himself a tentative deadline of early December before returning to meet with RSE again.

"Good afternoon Mr. Hughes. Would you like your usual?"

Damian glanced over the menu to find Adrianna smiling down at him. She'd served him for most of the week. Today he hoped to finally see....

"Imani." He whispered internally commending himself for selecting the perfect seat. She walked in, almost running, and slipped behind the bar area, disappearing into an adjoining room.

"Sir?" He exhaled a measured breath looking up into her questioning eyes.

"I'm sorry. Yes, the same and add a glass of water."

He closed the menu and placed it in her outstretched hand. The chatter in the bar was noticeably louder as more patrons filled the cozy space. Honestly he didn't want another turkey club sandwich, but he needed time to see the woman who'd captured too much of his mental space.

Adrianna walked toward the kitchen and Damian sat back and watched Imani. He had arrived in town Monday along with his assistant Mason. And for the past five days Damian arrived at least an hour before their scheduled meeting hoping to see Imani in person. He glanced at his watch; he had almost an hour before Mason's arrival, which gave him time to observe her without interruption.

He leaned back in the booth turning to hide his face in the shadows. Damian earned a moniker—The Shark. He never agreed with the predatory likeness associated with it. It wasn't attractive, but spine tingling and centered on his approach. His strategy started with learning his clients inside and out, not through private detectives. He gathered intel personally. His hands-on approach gave him the agility to move unseen, unheard, covered in an element of surprise.

This commission was no different. He started with the file from RSE, but from this moment forward it would be all first hand knowledge.

Imani stepped from out of the backroom and leaned over pecking Adrianna on the cheek. Today her hair was pulled up into a ballerina bun showing her perfect oval face exposing her elegant neck in a button up black dress shirt that complimented the golden brown hue of her flawless skin.

His pulse quickened, dropping his gaze to his hands pushing papers from one side of the table to the other. It had been months since he entertained a woman. His plans to invite Nicole to a no strings attached dinner while in Atlanta were thwarted because he couldn't seem to keep Imani's sexy pout from crossing his mind at the most inopportune times.

Talking with his parents. Conducting a meeting. Touring property. It was the damnedest thing. He glanced back over as she talked with a couple sitting a few tables over.

"Her name is Imani."

He nodded not taking his eyes off her as Adrianna sat the round paper coasters on the table with a cup of steaming hot coffee and iced water, leaving as quick as she appeared.

Damian had to close the deal and stop wondering if her mouth was as sweet as it appeared. He had a little over a month before he had to return to Atlanta. He sipped his black coffee and pondered the best offer to make Imani move out of the building without unwanted publicity. And get out of town before he did something insane like seducing her on the tabletop.

"Stop staring at the man and say something?"

Imani found working with Adrianna at the bar worse than working at the studio. At least at the studio she could pull rank and kick her out the office.

"What man?" She let out a long audible breath.

"The man that has you spilling drinks and stepping on my toes."

"Ouch!" She stomped on Imani's foot and wiggled out of reach.

Imani had been preoccupied with trying to see the features of his face. The booth he selected was tucked away off to the side. The overhead lights barely illuminated the tabletop. It was the table repeat customers chose when they wanted to partake of the live music and robust menu and have privacy.

It was public yet private. So private they'd witnessed more than one heated exchange going on in that booth over the length of her employment. It wasn't called the make-out booth for nothing.

Imani stole glances at him for most of the afternoon. She could see the top of his arm covered in a white dress shirt and the swirled tattoo on his forearm. That must be his girlfriend. She reasoned as the olive-skinned brunette took her sit across from him.

"You think that's his girlfriend?" Imani whispered. Adrianna topped off the customer's soft drink and walked over to stand beside her.

"If she's not, she wanna be." She dried her hands on her apron.

Imani faced her, "What makes you say that?"

"That man is a sexual magnet, paid with a Titanium Card, and his eyes," she shook her head and raised her hand in the truth, "panty droppers."

"For real?" Imani hissed. The forced air behind panty made curiosity dance through her veins.

"For. Real." She glanced over at the table as if validating her statement. Her face twisting in agony and she nodded.

Imani glanced back over there. The last thing she needed was to stare into his panty-dropper eyes. She wanted to ask Adrianna more but a warning voice in her head told her to leave it alone.

There was no room in her life for men. Life was hectic enough without adding sexy, magnetic, panty-dropping men to the equation and her panties needed to stay in place. The last man she'd given her heart passed her up for a bigger fish and left her without so much as a blink of an eye. Her time was better spent trying to find another job.

"Have you heard from your landlord?"

"I got a letter about a new owner. But they didn't mention the balance and I didn't either. I sent what I could, hoping it will hold me over."

$1250 a month times six months left her owing the

new landlord at least $7,500. It might as well have been a cool million because she didn't have a hundred dollars to her name. She hated owing people.

She was ashamed to admit what she sent barely covered the late fees but she still had to pay the utilities at the studio on top of her own household expenses.

"How long you think that's going to last? You can't keep doing this to yourself. This dance studio is like a leech draining you dry."

"Why would you say that? What's wrong with giving my students culture?" Imani stiffened at her harsh analogy.

"Ain't nobody got time for that!" She turned to Imani tossing a towel in the sink. "Culture won't feed you and pay your bills."

Tears stung her eyes. But she didn't have time to cry or feel sorry for herself. She needed a plan.

"Is he cute?" It was better to talk about the panty dropper than her landlord.

It was Adrianna's turn to shrug, "He's alright for a white boy. You know I like my *papi chulo* sun kissed, bilingual, and Spanish in his blood. Can't have my momma passing out on me."

"Indeed, your mom would pass out if you brought anything but a Hispanic man home." Imani laughed.

"That's why I keep my business *my business*." She

tossed her blonde hair and headed to the other end of the bar to check on a customer.

Adrianna talked a good game but she had a man. Her traditional ways went to her core from cooking authentic Mexican food to Salsa dancing every Thursday night. Imani looked back at his exposed skin, it didn't look white but not brown either. More like a warm beige. His head turned in her direction and she felt trapped. Unable to look away, but unable to see his face either.

The young lady returned to the table and Imani spun around, facing the mirrored wall behind the bar. She glanced up into the reflection and watched him lean forward. The light caught his profile with his thick wavy dark brown hair. He smiled up at his companion.

Imani's stomach clinched. He had a deep dimple.

She watched the young lady leave the table carrying her purse and shoulder bag. They must be done for the afternoon. She wanted to see this mystery man for herself.

She couldn't just stroll over, that would look too suspicious. Imani started a fresh pot of coffee and placed a clean mug on the bar, she'd offer him a cup of coffee. While the coffee dripped at a snail's pace she cleaned her area, swept the floor and went to the back to get clean glasses. She normally had to run out at four o'clock on the dot to get to the studio but it was Saturday.

"Hey, can you help me next week? I need help at the studio. The kids are out for Thanksgiving."

"I can't. Sebastian is taking me to meet his parents. Sorry." Adrianna grabbed the tray of food and headed in the opposite direction.

"I'll figure something out." That seemed to be her motto. Imani put the broom and dustpan back in its spot and rubbed her hands down the front of her apron. She'd been working doubles all month. Opening and closing. Today she would work straight through closing.

Holidays were hard for her. Her students were out of school and to accommodate their schedules she remained open all day. Her attendance increased by at least half. Some days it felt like money would solve everything. She could pay the rent, hire staff, and breathe a little easier. She glanced over at the coffeemaker just as the last few drops fell in the pot. Imani poured coffee into the mug as Adrianna returned.

"Where are you going?" Adrianna's face held a knowing smile.

Imani tilted her head towards his table. "Then break. I need some fresh air."

"How long do you expect to keep juggling everything?" The concern in her voice stopped Imani, Adrianna shook her head obviously not pleased.

"As long as I need to. First Thanksgiving. Then I'll sit down and think of something more concrete. I'm taking it one day, one event at a time. And don't worry so much."

"I would if you worried at least a little." Adrianna huffed.

Imani smiled and kissed her best friend's cheek glad to have someone concerned for her. She circled the bar and grabbed the warm handle of the cup, taking measured steps careful not to shake the cup too much.

Why was she tempting herself? The magnetic pull she felt from across the room radiated to full blast with each step.

"Should we start charging you rent?" Imani lowered the mug to the table focused on not spilling the hot liquid. The warm tone of his laugh made her heart race, glancing up she laid eyes on the man of the hour.

She was in trouble.

Continue Reading...

**Get Your Copy on Amazon
or Read in Kindle Unlimited!**

Blazin' Love (Contemporary Romance)

Platinum Love (Book 1)

Privileged Love (Book 2)

Exclusive Love (Book 3)

Chosen Love (Book 4)

Special Love (Book 5)

Absolute Love (Book 6)

Pretend for Me (A Short Story)

Devoted Love (Book 7)

Conspiracy Ink Series (Romantic Suspense)

Veiled Conspiracy (re-release Summer 2019)

Forbidden Chords Series (Contemporary Romance)

Rockstar Secrets (Book 1)

Rockstar Sinners (Book 2)

Rockstar Savages (Book 3)

Waiting for You (A Short Story)

This Song's for You (A Short Story)

Precious Stones Series (Romantic Suspense)

Before Black Diamond (Prequel)

Black Diamond (Book 1)

African Emerald (Book 2)

Fire Opal (Book 3)

Ready for Love Series (Sweet Romance)

Caramel Surprise (Book 1)

Love's Hope (Book 2)

Hidden Desire (Book 3)

Ready for Love Boxed Set (Books 1 - 3)

Smith Pact Duo (Contemporary Romance)

Yuki's Luck (Book 1)

Tempting Asher (Book 2)

Smith Surprise (Book 3)

When It Comes to Love Boxed Set (Books 1 - 3)

See all of my books on my website:

http://www.janesedixon.com/books.

ABOUT JA'NESE

Ja'Nese Dixon pens tales of romance in several sub-genres. But her favorites are the ones that manage to keep readers sitting on the edge of their seats lying to themselves about reading "just one more chapter".

Ja'Nese is an avid reader and coffee drinker, who also loves to run, cook, and craft. Her ultimate goal as a writer is to give you a little "staycation" with every story. And she aims to make this present story no exception. Sit back, grab a snack and enjoy.

Ja'Nese calls Houston home with her husband, three kiddos and a four-legged diva dog.

Visit her website at www.janesedixon.com if you enjoy romance, suspense and good stories.

Subscribe to Ja'Nese Newsletter "Reader's Staycation" for reader exclusives, regular giveaways and more.

Stay in Touch:
www.janesedixon.com
info@janesedixon.com

facebook.com/AuthorJaNeseDixon

twitter.com/janesedixon

instagram.com/authorjanesedixon

amazon.com/author/janesedixon

bookbub.com/authors/ja-nese-dixon

ABOUT THE PUBLISHER

Purpose Prevails Publishing
2231B Center St. STE 144
Deer Park, TX 77536